By Starlight

By Starlight

A Novel

Jimmy G. Mai Morillon

Mai Damn Self Publishing

Copyright © 2025 by Jimmy G. Mai

All rights reserved.

ISBN: 979-8-218-63564-0

Book Design by Jimmy G. Mai

www.jimmygmai.com

For the star that burns ever bright in my mind, my heart, my soul, and in my very essence of being. My darling, beautiful little sister, Crystal. You burn brighter than any star in the universe. I carry your light with me everywhere I go.

Table of Contents

Acknowledgements

Many like to say writing is a solitary act and while it is, publishing is a whole other beast and there are so many people I would like to thank who helped me on the road to getting this book out to you, the reader.

Ana Zermeno, my wife and who is my biggest champion when it comes to my writing and the translator of my books into Spanish. My mother Leticia Morillon, who gave me this insatiable desire to read and write and has always encouraged me to do what was best for me. My father Hien Mai for always planting me in the real world and teaching me how to fight back against it. My sister Cynthia Evans, who encouraged me to do it Mai Damn Self (Pun intended). My aunt Mireya, who has always been there for me on the best and worst days of my life. My cousin Victoria Santiago who has always read my work since our days at UHD.

Doug Seliger, my editor and only person I trust to change a sentence for me without letting me know. Tiffany Ma who also pushed me to do it Mai Damn Self and reminded me that if anyone could do it, it was me. Ann Rich, who read from front to end the final version of this draft. Troy Ward for all his advice and allowing me the use of "My Damn Self" for the publishing name. Gerardo Cardenas, thank you for the amazing author photo session. Lety Baskin whose strength passed over to me during the time that I was working on brining this book to publication, who is living proof that yes, you can do it your damn self.

To all my friends and family, thank you for your support and putting up with me.

Part One: The Evil

Without

What is the word to describe when a star that shone so bright suddenly goes out, without a flash or a thunderclap? A black hole remains, but the light is extinguished. What is the word used to describe a warmth that envelops every part of your heart and soul, suddenly gone cold without so much as a shudder? The blood still moves throughout your body, but your heart beats without meaning. What is the word used to describe a happiness taken for granted, suddenly stripped away, forcing you to see that you were in the good times and now those good times are over? The memories fade, but their shadows terrorize your every waking moment. You wish to forget them but realize that to do so would erase that light, that warmth, that happiness forever. Nothing is the same. Nothing *can* be the same. The only constant for the rest of your life will be pain.

Thoughts like these might have run through her mind, had she been able to articulate what she was feeling. Right now, however, the little girl wandered through her house calling for Mama and Papa and her older brother. No one answered her calls. No one would.

She awoke with only the sunlight to guide her, sneaking in narrow streams through shaded windows, casting its rays upon clues that she couldn't even know to look for. At eight years of age, she was old enough to know things but too young to notice—and what she knew was that she was alone.

She had no reason to suspect that they wouldn't be back. At least, not until the next day, when the sun rose again and she called for Mama with a lump in her throat. That day would come tomorrow. Today was still, after all, day one.

Chapter One

"Mama."

The silence was the first thing she noticed when she woke up, piled underneath a heap of blankets that she didn't remember using.

"Mama," she called out again, standing in the hall of their small home. The white walls absorbed her words as the cold tile enhanced the chill that crawled up over her body. The dim light creeping through the shades offered guideposts through the encroaching darkness.

A third time: "Mama."

That time, she knew something was wrong.

She recalled the way Mama would come out of her room, either smiling or scowling, depending on the tone of the voice that had summoned her. The girl would remember the scowls far less than the smiles. The smiles were all that she wanted to see right now, there in the darkness and silence that had taken over her home.

Silence. Darkness. Fear.

Fear swelled in her heart, fear that was already there on account of the coming war. Her parents talked about it every day. It wasn't there yet but it was coming, she remembered Mama saying over and over again. Papa, who couldn't fight because of his back, always reassured her.

"Don't worry. We're going to win, the Americans always win."

This same old conversation was the one that always played out when Mama told Papa that it was time to leave, to flee and try to get on a ship to the Philippines, that every minute that they wasted brought them one minute closer to death.

The girl walked timidly into the kitchen, hoping to hear her family having the same old argument, careful not to awaken an evil that she sensed lurking in the shadows—an evil that had seemingly sucked the sound from her home.

Where light usually poured in, there were now only narrow beams that pierced the oppressive darkness. Where was her family? Where was breakfast? Where was the warmth of the light of day? Where was Mama's smile? The gentle kiss on the top of her head from Papa? Her older brother's laughter as he joked that he already ate her food? Where was her family? Where was her life?

She planted her feet and closed her eyes, trying to force herself to wake up from the nightmare she was clearly having. Her little eyes clamped shut, her thin lips pressed together, her tiny fists clenched at her sides, her legs locked as she commanded her body to wake up.

Instead of waking up to another, warmer reality, she was taken back to earlier this week, when Mama and Papa were arguing again about leaving. This would be the last time.

"We have to leave. The Americans have *lost*." Mama's voice was filled with cold desperation, engendered by the Americans who had once promised them salvation.

"Where are we going to go?" Papa slammed the table in frustration. He had been wrong; they should have fled earlier, and now it was too late. The little girl knew that. She remembered standing in the hall listening with her older brother, who was scared too. They held each other's hands; it would be her last memory of him.

"Anywhere! We can't be here when they come!"

"Everyone is trying to leave. There's nowhere to go!"

"Let's go to the coast. The Navy will take us."

"The Navy's already gone. Anyone with half a brain has already left."

She remembered how Papa said that, realizing that he had not even half a brain because he had kept their family there.

"Well we can't stay here. It doesn't matter if we're still in the country, but we can't be in Saigon when they take it over. They'll kill you for the things you wrote. They'll kill *us* for the things *you* wrote!"

They weren't in the room when it happened, but she and her brother heard the chair screech back across the tile floor. They heard Papa take two quick steps towards Mama, they heard him slap her, they heard her fall against the table, they heard her crying, and they heard him scream at her.

"You don't think I know that?!" He threw something, glass shattering as they hugged each other trembling in the dark hallway, neither daring to cry. "You think I don't know that I've killed us? I do! I know! There's nothing to do. I will offer them my neck freely, but I can't control

13

what they do to you. You don't think it keeps me up at night? You don't think I want to go into the middle of town and denounce myself and shoot myself in the face so you all can live?"

Another glass shattered. He stomped away from her and wept quietly.

They had never seen Papa cry. Even now, they only heard it.

The memory faded as fast as it had come, and silence greeted the girl once again. A chill ran down her back, and instinctively she stood on her toes, looking for a sign that she might have missed. A note explaining where they had gone, an empty carton of milk on the table that they had quickly gone out to replace before breakfast, a sign that her trickster brother had concocted this whole scheme and everyone would jump out of their hiding spot as soon as her lip started to quiver.

She stood there silently on her toes, waiting for her world to come back to her. Except it never did. Her family was gone, and she didn't know why.

The kitchen was exactly as it normally was outside of mealtimes. The table was empty and clean; no dishes had been set. None of the fruit in the bowl had been disturbed, like it would have been if her brother or Papa was impatient and had to eat something to quell the beast growling in their belly. There was no folded newspaper at the head of the table for Papa. There was nothing except a room waiting patiently for a family to begin their routine.

Only the girl had shown up, and the girl wasn't so much eager for breakfast as she was for the family who had vanished without her.

She lowered her feet, let her lip quiver, and began to whimper as tears streamed down her face.

***

The kitchen was the first of many places where she would cry alone as fear overtook her heart. Her brother's room was next. Nothing was suspicious there, except that the bed had not been made. That was the only thing that offered her any clue; an untidy bed, which would never be allowed by Mama, meant that he had gone to wherever he had gone to in a hurry. She stood there, staring at the empty bed and thought *What about me?*

The girl immediately dashed to his dresser, pulling open each drawer to see if what she feared was true. *Did they escape to America without me?* her mind screeched over and over as she checked to see if her brother took his clothes.

Relief swept over her as she saw all his clothes in place, untouched. He hadn't taken anything, so they didn't leave her for America. They couldn't have. Relief was quickly replaced by fear once again, and she scurried to her parents' room next, her feet pattering against the cold tile, the only sound in a home where silence was once a luxury.

Like her brother's room before, the only thing amiss in her parents' bedroom was the unmade bed. Knowing Mama's incessant dedication to cleanliness, however, it was cause enough for grave concern. The sheet lay crumpled and twisted in the middle of the mattress, as if both of her parents threw their side off at the same time before running off to another room.

Hers was the only room that differed from the rest. She had crawled out from under a heap of blankets, blankets that weren't there the night before. They were all folded, except for the one she was sleeping directly under. The stack was four or five high, and she recognized them from the linen closet in her parents' room. They had been stacked directly on top of her, like they were meant to hide her.

She stared at the blankets in utter confusion. After a few dumbfounded moments, something finally clicked in her young mind; she had been deliberately hidden, which meant that she had been deliberately left behind as well.

Finally, a single sound pierced the silence—a ticking, echoing down the hall from the living room. She followed the sound until she came to the old clock hung high on the wall above her, forever out of reach. At just under four feet, the whole wide world towered over her. The ticking clock reminded her just how small and alone she was.

The sound comforted her, the steady clicking of the unseen gears the only certainty she could rely on now. Time continued flowing steadily forward, and she would have to as well. Staring at the moving hand, she remembered Papa's watch. It had a black face with khaki hands, silver frame, and a brown band. He'd had it for as long as she could remember. Like the flow of time, the sight of it on his wrist was constant. She stared at the clock in a daze, no longer crying. She relaxed her body and let out a

15

small breath, as if she were just released by some unseen force, and walked quietly back to her parents' room.

On the nightstand sat her father's watch. She picked it up and looked it over, examining the worn leather. She lifted it up and sniffed it, hoping to catch Papa's familiar scent, but all she could smell was stale sweat. She turned it over, poring over every little scratch, ding, and tick that it had acquired over years of use. The fact that he had left it created more questions, but confirmed once again that she was left behind.

The air around her stopped moving as she clutched the watch in her hand. Her heart came to such a gentle standstill that one would almost think it had stopped altogether. A coldness came over her, one that tightened her chest and enveloped her like she was sinking below an icy pond. She stared at the watch, nearly hovering by her parents' unmade bed.

The strap had no adjustment holes that would allow it to be tightened enough to accommodate her narrow wrist, but she took the watch with her all the same. Maybe she could give it to him when he comes back, she thought, not knowing that he never would.

Mama's jewelry lay where she had carefully stored it on her vanity. The mirror, framed with white wood, was rather small, but everything there was organized just so that despite how much she had, it all lay neatly in its own place ready to be picked up for whatever occasion, big or small.

It was all still there, down to the last jeweled earring.

She picked out a particular pearl necklace and the accompanying set of earrings, the set that Mama always happened to catch her playing with. She was not yet old enough to be allowed to pierce her ears, and Mama always scolded her when she caught her at the vanity. In fact, there was only one time that the girl had ever been allowed to put on Mama's pearls.

***

It was around springtime last year. The girl had been sick with a fever for quite some time. There wasn't a lot to go around in terms of food and medicine because of the war, but her family did have some money and scraped together something that at least kept the fever at bay.

16

The girl would lay in her bed, sweating from every pore in her body, her bones and joints aching whenever she had to move for one reason or another.

Mama came in one day when the girl was feeling just a little bit better, when there was a glimmer of hope that she would pull through and leave the sickness behind her after three brutal days.

Mama smoothed back the girl's damp black hair and touched her forehead. "I think your fever is finally breaking. Are you hungry? Do you want some water?"

She shook her head. Three days of fever had left her decimated; the only thing she wanted to do was lay there.

Mama clicked her tongue, a worried looked on her face. Suddenly her eyes widened slightly; she had an idea. She kissed her daughter's forehead and said, "Mama will be right back." She floated off the bed gracefully, a smile on her face, confident that what she had planned would perk her daughter right up.

Mama returned to the room shortly, holding her hands behind her back, smiling the smile she got whenever she had a sweet treat for her children or a plan to take them out somewhere fun for the day.

"Mama has something for you." She stepped in slowly, building the anticipation. "Can you guess what it is?"

The girl shook her head as a smile began to pull at the corners of her mouth. "No," she barely uttered out. "What is it?"

"You have to sit up if you want to see it."

The girl sighed, but she was curious. Using her elbows, she gingerly lifted herself up. The pain in her body, though it had lessened, was still there to remind her that she was quite ill.

Mama sat in the center of the bed, inching closer to the child as her clammy body rose to an upright position, eager to see, a sense of curiosity that even fever couldn't deter.

Satisfied that the girl had moved, Mama let her smile grow as she brought her delicate hands before her. The girl remembered how soft they were when the caressed her cheeks or held her, how they looked like silk clouds that day as they turned over and opened to revel the pearl necklace.

The pearls had done the trick; the girl smiled from ear to ear, forgetting the pain of the fever. She smiled sweetly at Mama, instantly filling the little room with the joy that had been missing while she was sick.

17

Mama nodded gently and held the pearls out. The girl lifted them up, smiling with her teeth. Mama undid the clasp for her and put them around her neck.

"They're healing pearls," she said. "They'll take away the fever so you can get better." The girl felt Mama's hand caress her neck as she straightened out her hair. "These come with a condition though," she warned, smiling as she lifted her daughter's face to hers. "You have to come eat something at the table."

The girl could feel the power of the pearls working on her skin already as her heart filled with Mama's smile. She nodded and took her mother's hand, and together they went to eat breakfast at the table for the first time in days.

***

Standing alone and holding the pearls in her hand, the girl remembered that day with a bright, loving haze around it. The power of those pearls radiated through her spirt once again as she stood alone in the house basking in the memory, and she felt less afraid.

Holding the pearl necklace and earrings gently in her little palm, she walked out of her parents' bedroom and back into the living room. She placed her father's watch neatly on the table, and then her mother's pearls beside it. Each was placed neatly and thoughtfully, in case her family suddenly came back and saw that she had been handling their things.

As if a bell went off, she shot up and dashed to her room where she leapt into her bed, burrowing underneath the mountain of blankets. For some thirty seconds she scurried and dug until finally she emerged with her prized possession: a stuffed white cotton rabbit.

With a smile on her face and the rabbit in hand, she trotted to her brother's room and threw open his dresser drawers, ransacking his clothes until she found a small red Swiss Army Knife. It was his prized possession, given to him by Papa on his birthday. She held it delicately in her hand and thought of her brother, wondering what he would say to her if he caught her in his room holding his only treasure.

With the rabbit and the knife secured, the girl pitter-pattered again to the kitchen and set all the items next to each other. For a moment, her family was together again in the spirit of all these things.

18

Silence again passed over her, save for the ticking of the clock in the living room. She glanced at it and back at the counter, and then decided what to do with her gathered treasures.

To her left at the small breakfast table, she placed the watch in front of Papa's chair. To its right, she gently laid the pearl earrings and necklace that Mama wore gracefully when going out or entertaining guests. In front of her, she placed her brother's Swiss Army Knife, its red lining shining in the sun. She made her way back to her own place at the table and neatly arranged her rabbit, as she had done for the other treasures.

She stepped back, careful not to make any noise, to not the disturb the family of items sitting at the table, three of them waiting for owners who would never return.

Chapter Two

The girl was lucky there was still food in the house that she could eat without cooking.

There was an assortment of fruit that she liked; crackers, rice cakes, noodles that she preferred to eat dry anyway, pork buns in the fridge that would hold for two more days, powdered milk, dried fruit, and dried cured meat and fish in abundance in the pantry.

It wasn't the steamed rice with meat and vegetables that Mama made, but it would keep her fed without having to teach herself to use the stove.

For her, it was a veritable feast. For a family of four living in a war zone, it was a rather lean allotment, one that Papa was able to sometimes bolster through dishonest means that Mama balked at—even as she accepted the goods when all they had was rice and a bit of fish.

She didn't understand what rations were, and she didn't understand why Mama had gotten so upset the first time Papa came home with meat when they hadn't had any in weeks. She thought it was a good thing. It sounded like Papa had done something dishonest or bad to get the meat, but she didn't know what. She just knew that Mama was scared the entire time and only got madder when Papa kept bringing home more and more food.

"You're putting us in danger," Mama said angrily one day while cutting a hunk of beef into strips.

"I'm keeping us from starving to death," Papa would reply as he sliced up a mango for her and her brother.

"The entire city is starving, the whole country is at war, and you're doing things for *them* so we can live like 'normal'," she said as she cast the thin slices of beef into a hot pan that hissed angrily at every ill-gotten piece.

"*They* are going to be the ones to win this for us, *they* are the ones giving us something real to eat." Papa stood up after he said this and walked over to her with a piece of fruit in his hand, holding it up. "Taste that and tell me it doesn't taste like victory."

The girl smiled at the memory, not at its content but at the vision of her parents. She felt her lip quiver; she hadn't quite gotten the hang of stifling her cries so when they came, the tears flooded out. She stood in the kitchen, holding a mango in one hand and a knife in the other, crying over not knowing. Not knowing where her family was. Not knowing what was going to become of her. Not knowing how to cut a mango.

***

After the sniffles passed, she cut the mango as best she could. She recalled the way Papa deftly wielded the knife, slicing the fruit in half before cubing it in its skin. He would hold it out to her and her brother, offering it up in such a way that the geometrical chunks of fruit emerged for them to eat straight from the skin with little effort. Satisfied, Papa would sit back, peel the skin back from the middle and chew the delicate meat of the fruit off its giant inner seed. His moustache glistened and eyes crinkled as he ate his favorite fruit with his children.

Using a chopstick to pin the rolling fruit down on the cutting board, she cut into it carefully so as not to hurt herself. Mama was always scared to let the girl help in the kitchen. Her fear was not unfounded; the first and only the girl had been allowed to help cut something resulted in a trip to the doctor and three stitches in her finger.

With considerable effort, the mango was cut successfully. She did her best to cube it like Papa always did for her and her brother, but the cuts weren't as deep in some places and the lines uneven. Still, the fruit was sweet, sticky and wet as it always was, and it brought her a little bit of comfort and hope.

Hope began to fill her heart as she ate. Hope that her family would return from wherever they had gone, either to take her with them or to once again fill this empty house that she had been crying alone in for an entire day now.

Chewing on the mango, she looked around the kitchen. Things were the same as they had always been, but the silence and emptiness of it all frightened her. Even with the early morning sunlight coming in and the sounds of the birds outside, it felt like a horror movie to her. She ate as noiselessly as possible and sat still as a statue, scrutinizing every single noise, giving each more importance than she ought to have.

21

A neighbor's door closed somewhere outside. A barely audible creak down the hall. The slow drip of the kitchen faucet. Each noise, completely innocuous before yesterday, now made her jump and shook her to the core.

This was the longest she had been alone in her life. The only other time she found herself alone was when she was left at the beach, but she was far too distracted with the wonders of the ocean to realize she had been left behind. Her parents noticed she was missing after they had driven away from the shore. Her brother knew but did not say anything because his parents were fighting. It wasn't until they came back that she realized she had been left and started to cry.

This time she knew they had left her, and all she could do was cry. The uncertainty of their departure left her bewildered and anxious. Without knowing their whereabouts, her fears multiplied, constructing an anxiety-ridden fortress in her mind With the war coming ever closer and the city growing more and more chaotic by the day, she feared both for herself and her family. If they had gone out into the city, were they in danger? Now that she was alone in the city, was she?

She ate the mango slowly, savoring its sweetness and delighting in the fact that she had cut it herself. With each bite she slowly allowed herself to be present in the moment. It was only when she was left chewing on the rind and saw the other half of the fruit waiting for her brother and the pit for Papa that she remembered she was completely alone.

Tears.

Her instinct was to call out, and it was here that she called out for Mama.

"Mama," she cried, holding the finished mango rind in her hand, juices caramelizing around her lips, her fingers leaving sticky prints on the table that Mama would have fussed about and made her wipe down. "Mama," she cried out again, her sobs carrying with them all the desperation that a child without her family could muster when all she wanted was to be held.

She looked around, hoping that her cries would cause Mama to suddenly reappear. Yet no one came. Mama didn't come out and put her arms around her and kiss the top of her forehead, nor did she click her tongue at the sticky mess she had made of herself. Papa didn't look up from his paper and pat her on the head, asking what was wrong. Her brother didn't make a nuisance of himself and tease her for crying. The only reply she got was the clock's mechanical ticking.

Instinctively, she wiped her face with the sleeve of her nightgown. The tears, crust from her eyes, the mucus, and the stickiness of the mango all came away after several wipes. Realizing what she'd just done, a reflexive anxiety came over her. She should have used a rag from the washroom, she'd been told by Mama over and over. She sat staring at her stained sleeve, still expecting Mama to come and scold her, roughly pulling the nightgown from her so she could wash it and sending her to the washroom to clean herself up properly. It was in these moments that the girl felt small, powerless, and afraid of the world that she lived in. Sitting there in the kitchen with her stained sleeve, she felt that mix of emotions creeping up around her, but they never fully materialized.

With Mama gone, the anxiety slowly subsided. The only thing she felt was the wetness of the sleeve hanging heavily from her pale, thin arm. Sniffling, she slid off her chair and walked to her room to change. For the first time in her life, she did this of her own free will and not because of Mama forcing her to do it, screaming and jerking her arms up to roughly remove the clothes she always so thoroughly ruined.

In her dresser drawers she found an array of clothing. Hesitating, she picked out a t-shirt that she always loved to wear. It was a simple white shirt with her favorite animal, Woodstock from Peanuts, on the front. She loved it, but Mama hated that she wanted to wear the same thing over and over again, so she always asked permission before putting it on, lest she hear the judgmental clicking of Mama's tongue.

Hesitation bubbled up in her once more as she held the shirt in her hand, but like the mixed feelings of shame and fear that briefly visited her at the kitchen table, it eventually died down. Satisfied that she wasn't going to get in trouble for staining her nightgown nor for wearing her Woodstock shirt, she snatched it and a pair of shorts out of the dresser and got changed.

***

She landed with a bounce in front of Mama's full-length mirror. Mama liked for her hair to be down and straight, but today she had it done up in a ponytail like she'd always wanted. Woodstock stood smiling on her shirt, staring at something off to the girl's right. The pair of denim jean shorts were chosen because they *felt* good rather than *looked* good. Rounding out the ensemble was a pair of black boots she convinced Papa to buy for her, but which Mama never let her wear outside. Satisfied with her chosen look, she smiled for the first time in a day as she skipped out of her parents' room and straight to her brother's.

Taking his Swiss Army knife and placing it at the kitchen table would have been enough to earn her a vicious hair-pulling. She wasn't allowed in the room with him, much less without him, and taking his things without permission was almost unthinkable. She loved her brother, but she also feared upsetting him.

But he wasn't here. When they showed up, she would shower him with love to make up for going through his things.

Squatting down, she peeked underneath his bed for hidden treasures. It was too dark to see anything, so she climbed onto the dresser and threw open the curtains to let the light in. Mama and Papa had always said to keep them closed, as the sunlight would heat up the house too much during the cool mornings.

But they weren't here either. So the light poured in.

Back to the bed, she again squatted and peered beneath to see what mysteries awaited her. Nothing. She frowned, disappointed that her brother kept no secrets or hidden treasures beneath his bed. She quickly realized, however, that neither did she. This was no place to hide anything, especially from Mama and her obsession with cleanliness.

Remembering the windows, she climbed onto the dresser again to close the shades. Before that, she did something she had not dared to do since she realized she was alone: she peeked outside.

Careful to not reveal herself in case anyone was watching, she poked her head slightly over the windowsill and scanned the area. She learned this behavior from Papa, who would stand at the window, cigarette in hand, peering through the side of the curtains in the living room, looking for something that only he knew he was looking for.

The top of her head sticking out slightly, the girl looked around only to see the neighbor's house. She didn't know what she had expected to see; the houses were packed so tightly together that the only view was of the neighbors' wall and its curtained windows. Dissatisfied, she pulled the curtains closed and stepped off the dresser slowly.

Back on the ground she scanned her brother's room and chose to continue her treasure hunt within the dresser itself.

The contents matched hers only in their neatness, minus the top two drawers which were now in shambles after she had searched for the Swiss Army knife the previous day. She went through each remaining drawer the same way, making sure to make a mess of things. Hopefully her brother would see what she did, and she would feel his anger. At least then she would feel something other than this empty silence that had enveloped her throughout the last twenty-four hours.

At last, she got down on her knees to search the bottom draw and…nothing.

Disappointed, she stood up and went to her brother's closet. Timidly, she pushed open one of its double doors. As she did with her own closet, she closed her eyes and kept them shut until both sides were open so she wouldn't have to see the unsettling darkness within. She groped for the second door and slowly slid that one open as well. Once she felt it stop, she stepped back, satisfied, and opened her eyes.

The contents appeared to be nothing spectacular. There were her brother's school uniforms neatly arranged, his social clothes, fancy outfits he never touched unless forced to by Mama. On the floor were the formal shoes that he seldom wore; his everyday shoes could be found by the front door, neatly arranged with everyone else's. On the shelf at the top of the closet were several boxes of things she couldn't directly see or reach. That's what she came here for. That's what she wanted to see.

Undaunted, she went to the kitchen to retrieve the step ladder Mama used to reach the higher shelves in the pantry and cabinets. It was a bit of a struggle for her to fold it closed and cart it off to her brother's room; it was almost as tall as she was, and a bit heavier than it looked. She remembered Mama pulling it out with her foot, grabbing it with one hand and snapping it open. The girl didn't think that she could do all of that, but she thought surely she could get it closed, carried over to her brother's room, and open again without much trouble. How wrong she was.

The whole ordeal took about thirty minutes. Getting it closed was the hardest part, but lugging it to her brother's room was also no small feat. She grunted as she walked, mimicking Papa whenever he had to lift something heavy. Finally, after many grunts and a bit of sweat, she stood atop the ladder, examining her brother's top shelf.

There were several boxes of knick-knacks that he had acquired, cheap toys from the local markets and a few nicer American toys given away by the soldiers. There was also a box of fireworks that he was hoarding. Some were colorful and enticing, others were solid red or solid black with an ominous acidic smell that made her nose crinkle. She was careful to put his things back after thoroughly examining them, but nothing really caught her eye.

After about forty-five minutes of rifling through his things, the only noteworthy items she'd found were a wad of cash that he had stashed, the fireworks, and an American soldier action figure which she took out to play with later. As she turned to climb down the ladder, something else caught her eye.

It was tucked away in the corner, in the very back, underneath a folded sweater that she hadn't bothered with. Taking the sweater and putting it to the side, she saw a small white and red box on top of what looked like a magazine. She reached as far as she could and managed to put her hands on the magazine, then carefully slid it towards her with the box on top. She grabbed it and stepped off the ladder, wanting to see whatever it was with proper light. Treasure in hand, she sat down at the foot of her brother's bed and examined what he had so carefully stashed away.

Cigarettes. She had seen these before. It was a red and white box with an American name she could not pronounce. She didn't really appreciate what she was holding until she realized the big trouble her brother would have gotten into if Mama had found the cigarettes instead of her. She had never seen her brother smoking; he probably knew she would have told Mama immediately. She opened the box and counted them. Eighteen. The box was mostly full and still looked new. The girl lifted one of the cigarettes to her nose and sniffed it, recoiling at the tobacco smell. It smelled old and stale, though she thought that might be the way they were supposed to smell.

She carefully placed the box of cigarettes down next to her, then focused her attention on the magazine. Another English name she didn't understand and didn't have to; the naked woman on the cover gave it away. She was holding a pornographic magazine.

The girl was curious to see what was inside, but remembering the way Mama screamed at Papa when she'd found a magazine like this in his things, she instead ran back to the ladder and returned it to its hiding place. She had never seen Mama so angry before, and she certainly did not want to risk being seen with such a magazine when her family returned. She replaced the sweater, crawled back down, moved the ladder, and closed the closet doors. Grabbing the cigarettes, she ran out of the room with her heart pounding.

Instinctively, she ran to her bedroom and dove underneath her bed, waiting for Mama to come storming in, somehow aware of the forbidden items she had found. Her heart thundered against her tiny chest, and she tried holding her breath to slow it down. She stared out from underneath her bed, clutching her brother's cigarettes, waiting for the wrath of the world to rain down upon her.

But it never came.

As much as she didn't want to be the subject of Mama's wrath, she had hoped deep down that finding the magazine would have been enough to summon Mama from wherever she'd gone, rampaging into the room, grabbing the girl by the wrist, and taking her over the knee with Papa's belt. She would have yelped out in pain and cried for hours after the spanking, but she would have also cried tears of joy for having Mama in the same room again.

As she waited for Mama to materialize out of nothing, her heartbeat steadied. Her panicked breaths turned into small, shallow ones and her fists unclenched as they gave way to the disappointment that grew and relaxed her hands.

Of course, Mama was not coming. "You're stupid," she finally said out loud to herself.

Hand over fist, she created a little mountain on which to rest her head. The tears came again, but this time her body didn't shudder with sobs like it had before. She watched a beam of sunlight slowly make its way across the floor of her bedroom, the white tile still sparkling from when Mama cleaned it the day before.

Mama cleaned it every day, she thought to herself as she cried silently on the floor. *Who was going to clean it now?*

It was then that thoughts of the future first intruded into her mind. *What am I going to do now?* she thought, watching the sunbeam mark the minutes that passed as she hid underneath her bed. "What am I going to do?" she whispered into the void.

***

She had fallen asleep for a couple hours, there on the floor. Her tears had pooled onto the tile and grown cold. It was the sudden cold wetness that woke her as her head moved slightly to reunite with the tears that left her little face as she slept, dreaming of Mama's loving voice, Papa's gentle caresses, and her brother's piercing laughter. She let herself forget Mama's shrill screech when she'd made a mess of her room, Papa's rough hands when she disobeyed him, and her brother's taunts when she would cower under him and his posturing. Those were things she would remember on the other side of that coin. For now, however, she only remembered the good times, because they certainly seemed to be over.

Her eyes wistfully gazed upon everything that they could from her hiding spot. The bottoms of her dressers, the feet of the bed, the door leading out into the hall. She would hide here sometimes, whenever her parents were fighting, watching the angry sandaled feet furiously walking back and forth from room to room, sometimes stopping to face each other and exchange heated words. These moments would make her laugh on the inside—for she would not dare to laugh out loud—because it looked as though the feet were yelling at each other.

Many times they would fight at the table, forcing her and her brother to bear witness to the nasty things they would say to each other. Oftentimes it started over nothing, but the fight would escalate into things that Papa was doing to put the family in peril, or how Mama was a bad wife in his eyes.

Some of the fights were different, but they always started the same; some outside thing that didn't happen at home would make its way in over fights that started there.

She huffed and was about to crawl out from underneath the bed when she heard it. A thud at the front door.

She stopped and listened, fear gripping her heart once again. She was home alone, she didn't know what to do if someone came knocking. Her mind raced thinking about who or what it could be. What if it was the army, come to drag her away like Papa always said was going to happen? What if it was a child abductor that Mama had always warned her about? What if it was her brother's friend, the one who always came over and tried to touch her down there when no one was looking? What if it was the

28

teacher at school who always hit the students' knuckles with a ruler whenever they were talking too much in class? The list went on and on in her mind as she silently listened for any more sounds.

After thirty more minutes of waiting and listening, she crawled out from beneath the bed, staying as small and quiet as possible, and ventured out to see what the noise could have been.

***

The package lay haphazardly on the doorstep. The way it looked—more of a bundle than a package, really—made it clear that it had been thrown there rather than placed carefully. The girl looked around quickly through the crack of the door. The sun shone brilliantly outside. She heard cars and motorbikes going by, but saw nobody in the neighborhood that would notice her if she stepped out.

With the speed of a frightened animal, she threw the door open, stepped out, retrieved the bundle, sped back inside and slammed the door shut. She stood against it, clutching the bundle, her mind racing and her heart pounding against her chest, wanting to explode.

Her little heart couldn't contain the excitement and fear that she had felt opening the door and stepping outside. Her mother had always been overprotective of her going out alone, especially with the war. There was no telling what anyone would do to a little girl her age during these uncertain times, Mama would always tell her, wagging her finger.

"You could go out and they'd snatch you up and we would never see you again. Is that what you want?" Ultimately, she would shake her head no and wait to go out whenever Mama or Papa could take her and keep a watchful and protective eye over her. Opening the door to retrieve that package was an ordeal for her, something Mama would have pulled her ear for and made her sit in her room for the rest of the day, reading books that she had already read five times over.

Standing there in the hall, recovering her breath and allowing herself to calm down, she smiled. It was the first thing she had done on her own in a long time, and as terrifying as it was, it was exhilarating. She looked down at the bundle in her hands and sighed. Now that she'd calmed down, she recognized what it was: letters from Papa's village,

29

correspondence from the front, and a newspaper that was still operating in town.

She walked over to the table and set it down, unraveling the string, taking care not to tear anything in case Papa came back. It would not do to tear his mail. All she wanted was the newspaper, anyway.

Her excitement grew again; she would be the first to read the day's news. When it came to the family pecking order, she was firmly at the bottom. Granted, she didn't understand a lot of what was written in the paper, but she still liked to do what her Papa, Mama and her brother did. This time, however, she was the only one here to receive the mail and thus, the first one to read the newspaper.

She went through the stacks of letters one by one. Many were from Papa's village, from her aunts and uncles. She only saw them once or twice a year, but they hadn't visited at all since the war started because it was too dangerous to travel. Luckily, they were all in the south and could still mail each other things, but with the war going on, travelling outside of the city was off limits.

Some of the letters were from friends here in the city. Papa wrote to them regularly even though they were local, because it was better to stay at home as much as possible. Besides, not many people wanted to be seen with Papa in the first place. He had said many things when it looked like they were going to win the war. Now that it wasn't looking that way, many people began to stay away from him out of fear. It was something that her parents argued about many times. Mama used words like "outcast" and "social piranha" but Papa kept saying "We're going to win, we're going to win" over and over again. He stopped saying it after Tet, when the North attacked everything at once. The girl didn't understand any of it, she just knew that the North attacked everything and that it wasn't fair.

After that, Papa's friends stopped coming over for coffee and important talks. Mama's friends stopped coming too. All of a sudden, she and her brother had no more friends to play with. They were all alone in a city where the war was coming, and people were afraid of who they could be friends with. The only ones they had were each other, and all they could do lately was argue and fight.

All in all, there were fifteen letters. One of them was a thick envelope from her aunt south of the city. She weighed it in her hands and tossed it up and down, wondering what it was and whether she should

30

open it or not. For now, she decided against it and instead picked up the newspaper, which she had coveted since she saw it by the door.

She smoothed it out, taking in the feel of the textured paper against her hand and the smell of the freshly printed ink. The characters all looked so official and important that she didn't take time to read any of it, only admiring the photos and the way the text was neatly arranged around them. She opened the paper, examining each page's design carefully as if they were works of art. She admired the photos, making up her own stories about what was happening in them rather than reading the text.

One photo showed a group of sad kids who had gotten together to pout about not having enough candy to eat. Another was a woman who was worried about whether her cat would come home. Many depicted soldiers who liked to squat in bushes and look at trees. The ones with Americans were staged Hollywood pictures used to promote the war so boys and men would join up (that one came from her father who refused to tell her what Khe Sanh was). One showed fish sleeping on the banks of the river, taking a break from swimming. These were the stories she told herself, the stories she made up, because she didn't quite understand all the words she saw in the newspaper.

When she was done with the pictures and the small comics section, she went back to the front page and at last read the big letters at the top.

"NO TRUCE."

The girl blinked a few times, trying to understand what the word "truce" meant. She struggled; she had heard it a few times before at school but could not remember what it meant exactly. It was the only two words on the front in big letters, so it was important.

Hopping off her chair, she scuttled to Papa's office where he kept all his important books. She knew she had seen a dictionary on his desk; maybe she could figure out what the word meant. Though when she'd tried looking up confusing words in the past, she found she didn't understand the words used to describe the word she wanted to define.

She hesitated in front of the closed door. She and her brother were forbidden from going inside there. It was his private space, and he didn't want them messing up his things. She took a deep breath and slowly opened the door, hoping that he hadn't been hiding in there all this time, ready to slap her across the face like he did when she walked in unannounced to tell him that dinner was ready.

31

The creaking of the worn hinges caused her to hesitate. Pushing the door further, she slowly craned her neck inside and examined the sacred place that only one person in the house was allowed to enter. The room was dark; it was on the side of the house where sunlight didn't come in naturally, and Papa always kept the shades drawn. She opened the door completely to let in as much light as possible.

The air smelled stale, like her brother's hidden cigarettes. In the middle of the room sat Papa's desk. It was simple, made of some specific kind of wood she couldn't remember but that he would always brag about to his friends. She and her brother were more focused on sneaking their way in, but they never made it through the door before Papa shut it in their faces as his friends settled inside.

Behind the desk sat a couch and two armchairs, surrounding a small coffee table. The girl walked by the simple desk, upon which were collected many books with titles she did not know and small sheafs of paper next to Papa's typewriter. She looked at the coffee table, water stains scattered across its surface, and noticed an ashtray in its center with a single, solitary cigarette butt snuffed out in it.

"*Ooh*," she let out, an acknowledgment that Mama would have been furious about what she'd found, but the girl quickly silenced herself. Her "ooh" had been enough to make her feel that she'd disturbed the sanctity of this place, and she chose to stay quiet. The feeling was as though she ran the risk of waking up someone, or something.

A chill crawled down her spine. How many times had her father sat in this room writing by himself, or talking with his friends about ideas that they eventually found so scary that they stopped coming over? The unknowns of the room filled her with a sense of dread.

Suddenly she felt the cold biting at her feet as if ice had engulfed them. She leapt back from the sitting area and shook off each foot, checking around her to see what could have caused such a cold feeling in the middle of a spring day, but she saw nothing. Standing there, alone, she felt the room grow frigid as the walls began to vibrate. Fear once again forced its way into her tiny heart, and she turned to run out of the room. She ran past the tall bookcase, the only other piece of furniture in her father's office, and slammed the door shut.

She collapsed against the door, heart pounding as she tried to overcome the fear that had taken her over. She didn't know what that feeling was or what happened in the room; all she knew was that she didn't like it and that whatever made the walls shake was bad.

Real bad she thought over and over again as her feet warmed and she waited to be sure that stillness again reigned supreme in the walls of her home.

She edged back into the kitchen, where light was shining full force now, illuminating the place where her family once gathered, and tried to soak up those feelings and memories that made her warm on the inside.

She sat in her chair, pulled her stuffed animal close to her, tucked her feet underneath her legs, shut her eyes and thought about her mother. The coldness in her feet gradually dissipated, the sunlight warmed her face, and the fear inside melted away as she remembered the love and care that was given to her and how it would be given to her now if only Mama were here.

Fifteen minutes passed, and finally she opened her eyes. They immediately went to the newspaper in front of her, and its big letters forming words which she did not understand. "NO TRUCE." She didn't know what happened in the office or what made her feel that way, all she knew was that she didn't like it and that she wasn't going back in there any time soon.

The dictionary and the word "truce" would have to wait.

Chapter Three

The office door stood before her, menacing in its normality, a simple portal to the evil that waited inside. She would stand in front of it, both scared and curious at what happened and what it contained. The girl didn't know a lot of things, but she knew what she knew: that whatever it was in there was bad, and more than that, it was Evil.

In fact, she officially dubbed whatever it was that scared her yesterday "The Evil."

She spent the entirety of the day, from breakfast to lunch and lunch to supper, walking to and from the door. Trying to find the courage to burst in there, grab the dictionary off the shelf, run out, slam the door shut and find out what the word "truce" meant, but she never did. The best she had done was to grab the doorknob, but retreated to the safety of the kitchen when she felt that cold rush into her body again.

When evening fell, she made sure the shades were drawn and the curtains closed before hunkering down in the fort she had built in the living room to defend herself against The Evil. Armed with a flashlight, her brother's Swiss Army Knife, her stuffed rabbit, and a frying pan that she could lift, she huddled amidst a fortress of pillows, chairs, and blankets. Inside, she had various pieces of dried meat, fruit, and noodles that she could eat uncooked.

For entertainment, she brought an assortment of books that Mama had read to her, as well as some of her brother's that she had not read yet. She also had the newspaper and the bundle of letters with which it had arrived.

The lamp next to the sofa made up part of the fort's foundation. Its light would remain off unless The Evil became too much for her, at which point switching it on would be a last resort. She didn't know for certain if it would keep it away, but all the scary stories she knew made it seem that evil hated light, and she had no reason to believe The Evil itself would be any different.

34

She clutched the flashlight in her hand. The sun hadn't quite gone down all the way, so there was still a bit of waning daylight in the living room. As accustomed as she had grown to the silence recently, the house still seemed eerily quiet.

There were no groans or creeks or slight pings, not even the ticking of the clock. The silence had consumed that sound as well. She sat in her fort among her comforts, waiting for that cold feeling and the fear to leave the office and encroach upon the rest of the house.

"Lamp lamp," she said to herself as she huddled in the darkness, waiting for The Evil to come so she could switch on the lamp at the last second and defeat the cold with light.

She thought again about the dictionary sitting in Papa's office. She clicked on the flashlight and looked again at the newspaper's headline. "NO TRUCE." She knew something was not to be, she just didn't know what. She clicked off the flashlight and turned to the stack of letters that came with the newspaper. The pile was hefty for her. She was most curious about the thick envelope that had something substantial in it. She wanted to know what it was.

There was still hope in her heart that she would see her family again, but there was also the feeling that it wouldn't be any time soon. She wondered how much trouble she would get into if she opened the mail. After all, they're the ones who left her. Why shouldn't she open the letters?

She probed one of the flaps on the top letter in the stack with her index finger, tracing the lines on the back where the envelope was sealed. She would understand what her family wrote a lot better than the newspaper, it was just a matter of reading it.

She sighed and put the letter to the side. It would be better if she waited for Papa, she thought. She didn't want him to be mad at her when they finally reunited.

Darkness had finally cast itself upon the house. For the last three nights the only source of light the girl used was the flashlight for getting around and reading books underneath the bed. She dared not turn on any lamps. She dared not alert anyone that she was here alone.

"The city is a dangerous place for little girls," Mama and Papa would tell her all the time. In her house all alone, she knew that a light would tell her neighbors that there was someone home, and if they had seen her family leave then they would know that it was she who was home alone, and they would come take her away and do horrible things to her, things that Mama never told her about specifically but assured her would happen.

The flashlight clicked on, and the small beam found its way to the office door. The girl was afraid of The Evil inside, but she was growing ever curious about what "truce" meant and was beginning to entertain the possibility of going back in there to find the dictionary and run out before The Evil had a chance to get her.

The flashlight clicked off, and the office door was once again shrouded in darkness. The girl could still feel it, even though she couldn't see it. It was calling to her. Her gaze never left it, her face never turned from its direction, never twitched or even moved a muscle. The Evil was in there; she knew it, and it was waiting for her to go in there again.

It knew that she wanted the dictionary, and it knew that her curiosity was getting bigger and bigger, knowing that what she needed was so close and also that there was something evil and scary in there waiting for her. She clicked on the flashlight again. The door was there, the same as it ever was and the same as it ever would be. Except now, it was waiting for her.

Inside her fort there was all the protection she needed. She had her flashlight, her rabbit, her brother's Swiss Army knife, the frying pan, and the lamp. In the office all she would have was her flashlight. The Evil would come out and overpower her and do whatever it was it wanted to do with her.

Or I can hurt it with the light, she thought. She looked down at her small flashlight. It was worth a try, she mused; she could go in, find the dictionary quickly, and if it came out she could throw light on it and hurt it, giving her a chance to close it in the office and escape to her fort where she would read the newspaper in peace with her flashlight and lamp at hand.

"What else am I going to do?" she said out loud, breaking the silence that had dominated her life for the last three days.

It was decided when the ticking of the clock made itself apparent again. She listened to it for a while gathering her courage, stood up, poked her foot out of the fort, and stepped out to meet The Evil.

***

36

She recoiled when she felt the stinging cold of the doorknob. Undaunted, she wrapped her hand in her t-shirt before trying again. The image of Snoopy and Woodstock crinkled as she turned the knob ever so slightly, so as to prevent The Evil from being alerted to her presence too quickly.

Slowly, the door opened. The girl let go of the freezing doorknob and stepped into what felt like an icebox. A random memory forced its way into her mind, one of Papa holding her up to the open freezer door so she could feel the cold.

She shivered. The flashlight beam entered the room, and for the first time in her life the girl saw what looked like a puff of smoke leave her mouth. She clutched at her face, having never seen such a thing before, but dropped her hand from her mouth when she realized that she was breathing fine. She blew into the frigid room and once again saw a puff of vapor. It was her breath freezing in the cold air, something that she quickly remembered hearing about in a book that Mama had read to her before bed once.

It was so cold in Papa's office that she could see her breath, something that both amazed and frightened her. The rest of the house was comfortable, but in here it was freezing. She swept the beam of light around the office wildly, hoping that if The Evil was in there, it would recoil in pain so she could get the dictionary.

Satisfied, she stepped into the room. Her skin pricked up with goosebumps, and she began to shiver as she walked further inside. Each step seemed to bring with it a drop in temperature.

Careful to avoid the area where Papa sat with his friends, she reached the bookshelf and wildly swung the flashlight behind her—just in case—before beginning to look for the dictionary in earnest.

She started with what was right in front of her, which was the middle shelf, and began scanning form left to right. The beam of light illuminated titles that she hoped to one day read so she could talk about them with Papa in his office, like he did with his friends.

The titles were foreign to her. She recognized words and letters but couldn't put them all together. The dictionary would be easy to find; it was white and orange and only said "Dictionary" on the spine. She moved to the second to last shelf, once again scanning left to right.

Her heart began to beat faster. She instinctively turned and slashed the light all over the room once again in case The Evil was about to get her.

Hands aching with cold, she returned to the shelf, bending her back to see the titles at her waist. The Dictionary shouldn't have been this hard to find. Had it been daylight she would have been able to simply look at the shelf and find it at a glance.

Nothing.

On her knees now, she shot a worried glance behind her, scanning the room again with the light before beginning to search the last row of books. Midway through, she felt the floor begin to rumble beneath her. Her heart began to pound, knowing that The Evil was coming out and she still hadn't found the dictionary.

Her palms began to sweat, and the sweat immediately cooled in the chilly air, feeling to her as if her hand would freeze around the flashlight. She began to shake from the cold and fear. The Evil sensed this, and the walls began to shake with the ground. She heard a rumble in the air, like a growling animal.

Filled with absolute terror, she jumped up and screamed, the flashlight flying out of her hand and landing with ironic grace on top of the bookshelf. She instinctively began to climb the shelf, both to get away from the rumbling floor and to retrieve the only weapon she had against The Evil that was now growling at her.

With reflexes like a cat, she clambered to the top shelf, grabbed the flashlight and wildly swept the beam around the room. Feeling herself losing balance, she quickly reached back to hold onto the shelf with both hands when she saw it—a flash of orange, the dictionary.

The girl put the flashlight in her mouth, grabbed for the book with her icy hand and leapt off the bookshelf. The floor was still shaking, the walls still trembled, and the growl grew deafeningly loud. Whether it was hungry or angry, she did not know, all she knew was that she needed to get out and she bolted for the door, slamming it behind her, running until she was safely within the thin-sheeted walls of her fort.

Clutching the dictionary in her hand, flashlight still in her mouth, she panted as she attempted to shake off the cold that had permeated her entire body. She felt the much warmer air on her skin, but the few moments she'd spent in that ice cavern that used to be Papa's office had chilled her to the core.

Taking the flashlight out of her mouth, she clicked it off and set the dictionary next to it. Sitting there in the darkness, she rubbed her hands and arms to shake the terror and the chill out of her body.

Her ears trembled, still echoing with The Evil's guttural roar. Her feet still vibrated from the shaking of the floor, her hands jittering from the frozen air. The violence that visited her in that room was a stark contrast to the relative peace of her living room fort. She wanted to cry, but the tears wouldn't come. They stayed frozen in her ducts, immobilized by fear of the unknown—of The Evil.

The clock's ticking seemed louder now that she was out of that room. She shivered again and cursed herself for allowing her curiosity to get the best of her. Still though, she accomplished her mission. She had the dictionary, and now she was able to find out what the word "truce" meant so she could figure out why it was important that there wasn't going to be one. She spent the better part of thirty minutes warming herself up, focusing not on The Evil but instead what she was going to read and whether or not she would open up the letters sent to Papa.

When at last she was warm and confident that The Evil would stay within the confines of the office, she turned her attention to the dictionary.

She turned on the flashlight with a gentle click, and like so many times before when she was under her covers with a book past bedtime, she began to carefully thumb through the dictionary's pages.

She thought of Papa, who taught her how to use the dictionary, and her brother, who taught her how to really find definitions when definitions gave you no real answers. She remembered the word "failure," which the dictionary defined as "to have failed." She was confused because she didn't know what "failed" meant. Frustrated, she began to cry, and it was her brother who taught her how to look for root words and find out what a word really meant.

Flipping through the Ts she felt sad, remembering that moment and wondering if she would ever see her big brother again. Though they fought many times and he often teased her, she missed his presence. She loved him as much as she did Mama and Papa, and she hoped one day to be near him again, as she did her parents.

She flipped past "trauma," another word she didn't know, and knew that she was getting close to "truce." Slowing down, she stopped flipping multiple pages and began to turn them one by one. After a few more turns she came upon the word that eluded her for a day, the one that caused her to go into a room that had become The Evil's home.

"Truce." She read the definition out loud. "An agreement to stop fighting."

The words left her lips softly, innocently, dissipating in the air like the collective hope of the people in her country. There would be no truce. There would be no stop to the war until the North won. She didn't need to look up any root words to understand that.

The girl closed the dictionary softly, laid it gently on the ground, clicked off the flashlight, and sat in the darkness. She knew that the war was coming to the city, to her, and her family wasn't here to protect her.

Once again, she cried in her loneliness. Her tears fell for the absence of her family, for the presence of The Evil lurking in her home, for the oppressive darkness enveloping her, and for the impending war descending upon her city, a war that threatened to disrupt her way of life much more than her family's absence had and in ways that she had never imagined. War was coming, she could really feel it for the first time, coming to swallow her up.

***

After crying her little eyes out, she picked up the stack of letters and, one by one, began to open them. She read about the horrors her family was facing, of the army advancing towards them, of starving, of losing loved ones, of people disappearing without a trace, the horror of losing everything, the reality of war.

The letters from her father's friends weren't sophisticated or intelligent like she imagined them to be. They were pleas for him to save himself, to take his family out of the city and find refuge with the Americans. Some were angry and urgent, others were fearful and loving, but all of them carried the same message: you must get out of the city.

She let the letters fall to the floor as she finished reading them, not bothering to put them back in their envelopes. Her family was gone and the war was coming. There was nothing to do. No one to fear. *It* was coming and there was nothing to do but wait for it to get there.

The last one she opened was the thick envelope, expecting to find a lengthy letter or some personal effects from family. What fell out, however, were four identical small white packages, bundled together. Confused, she looked at the envelope to see who had sent them. There was no address, simply the surname of their family: Nhat.

It was a name that now belonged to her alone. While they all had their "first" names which came last and they all used, she was the only Nhat left in this house, and she decided to take the name as her own.

Nhat took the four small packages, examining them and lining them up. Each had one family member's name on it. She arranged them in order, starting with her father, then her mother, then her brother, then her.

Each was a little bit bigger than a deck of cards and about as thick as four of them stacked up on top of each other. They were tightly packed and, upon closer inspection, wrapped several times with clear packing tape. The names were written on them with black marker.

Nhat picked up the fourth package, hers, and began to unravel the tape. It was well-packed and sealed tight, taking her the better part of an hour to unwrap. She struggled to find where edges began, and some of the tape came up with other layers, creating tangles of thick plastic that she had to gingerly cut using her brother's Swiss Army knife. In the end, she was left with the white packing paper that was held together with a single piece of scotch tape.

Without ceremony, she removed the tape and unfolded the paper to reveal its contents.

***

There was something unsettling about the piece of paper that had her name and face on it. She recognized the photo; it had been taken by her father one day when he brought home a camera he had borrowed from a friend. It was fancier and more expensive than the one they had at home, so she and her brother were forbidden from touching it.

They each took an individual photo before coming together to take a family picture. This was the explanation her father had given them for borrowing the expensive camera—so they could have a nice family photo.

41

"We need to get all the seriousness out, get all the meanness out of our faces so we can have a photo together where we are all happy," he told her when she asked why she wasn't supposed to smile. Satisfied with this explanation, she did what he asked and stood silently against the wall for a serious, non-smiling picture.

That was the picture staring back at her now, on a card with all of her information on it. Her full name, her birthday, the address of their home, how tall she was, the color of her eyes and hair, everything someone would need to know to make sure it was her.

After that, there were many pieces of paper that she didn't understand, four copies of each. Two of them were tickets, one of which she recognized immediately as for a boat. A couple of years ago on an outing, she and her family had gotten on a leisure boat and went around the South China sea. It was a fun day; she ran around on the deck with the seagulls while Papa and her brother fished. She helped Mama make banh mis for lunch and played with kids from the other families. The sun was out. The water was blue. Everyone smiled that day. No one fought.

The ticket in her hand made her happy, but also sad. If these packages were all the same, that meant everyone else had their own ticket but weren't here to claim it and wouldn't get on the boat with her and have a fun time like last time.

The other ticket she didn't recognize but figured it must have been for an airplane ride because of the plane in the corner, pointing up as if it were lifting off into the air. She scanned the ticket as best she could, but it was all in French and she couldn't make heads or tails of it. The only thing she did recognize was her name, which stuck out against the French words like a sore thumb.

The remaining documents were all too complicated for her to read. One was in Vietnamese and she couldn't understand anything except for words like "the," "and," "if," and the other basic words connecting the complicated ones together. One of them had an eagle on it, holding arrows and leaves. The letter itself was in a language that had no accent marks and looked kind of like French, but the words seemed stiff and hard, as if they had died and fallen together onto the paper. Another was in French, which she did understand a little, but without a translation dictionary would probably be unable to read. Each of these came with four copies as well.

Finally, there was a letter that had been typed on a typewriter, seemingly from the person who sent them all of this. This she was able to read without having to look up any words. It was short and simple, and it terrified her beyond anything because she realized what she had to do after she read it.

Chi Chien,

You're approved to enter the United States from the French Embassy. The US has agreed that you provided valuable intelligence, and will grant you asylum. Hell, I think they're getting everyone out that they can at this point. But listen—you have to get out of the country first and take a plane from Hong Kong to France. You've got passage to the Philippines, but I couldn't get you a ticket from there to Hong Kong. You will have to take care of that yourself. I've included enough money for you and each of your family members to get there and to have enough to eat.

Everything you will need is in these packages. I've included four copies of everything except the tickets, but do not carry them all in one bag. Keep one set on your person, one set in a backpack, another in a piece of luggage, and leave one set in your home in case you get sent back and must start over. Do what I did with one set and wrap it up tight in tape, so it doesn't get wet. I would make sure the plane ticket is wrapped in that set, so you don't have to worry about it.

Don't carry everybody's documents yourself, either. If you get separated, I have arranged it so each of you can get into the US alone, if needed. Keep an eye on your daughter, she might be the only one who would need help. You, your wife and son can manage. Make sure that one of you is always with her.

You must *leave no later than two days after you receive this package. You may have to wait around in Hong Kong for a little bit, but that's ok. The more time you have to spend there means that you didn't face any trouble getting out. I've arranged it so that you have some wiggle room in case things don't go smoothly. If you wait longer than two days to leave, I can't guarantee that you'll make it in time. Take whatever is most important—try to keep it to one piece of luggage per person—and get the hell out. Take as much food as you can that won't spoil; you don't know what it'll be like in the Philippines.*

By the time you get this, I'll already have left. I'm including the address where I will be staying in France, come find me when you get there. You will stay with me and my family.

Thank you for everything. I hope this makes us even.

Farewell brother,

43

I will see you soon.

The letter was unsigned, but she knew that it was from her uncle who lived farther south. Nhat read it over and over again, half wondering what to do and half knowing that this was her only chance to escape the war that was coming—and The Evil that was already here.

She began to cry.

Nhat had everything she needed to get out of the country, but like her uncle had written, the enormity of that task seemed to be too much for her.

She would have to escape the city on her own. She would have to get on the boat on her own. She would have to get to the Philippines on her own. From there, she would have to figure out how to get to Hong Kong by herself, fly to France, find her uncle, and somehow make it to the US like her family had planned. Maybe she could just stay with her uncle, she thought. All the same, she would still have to do all those things on her own.

The thoughts wondering what she should do turned quickly into thoughts of whether or not she could even do it. The war was coming, and The Evil was already here, lurking. She had to leave and follow the plans her father and uncle had set up for them. The question now was: could she do it?

Cross-legged, she set the letter down in her lap. She looked out into the darkness of the house, the faint glow of the flashlight against her tan legs casting her fort in an orange light. She had felt lonely and afraid for the last three days, but only now, after reading this letter and understanding what she had to do, did she truly feel alone.

A terror seized her throat. She wanted to cry but the tears wouldn't come. Realizing the reality of her situation and the danger she was in, her body seized up. From this moment on, every decision she made could be her last.

Looking out of her fort towards the door, she thought about the terror that awaited her outside of her home and considered The Evil that lurked within it. "I can die outside, or I can die inside," she said out loud, the last vestiges of her innocence floating away with the words.

Though a child, she was now saying goodbye to her childhood. That kind of innocence belonged to those for whom it would not be a

44

liability, and whether inside this house which sheltered The Evil or outside with the war bearing down on her, that kind of naivete could get her killed. She was at the end of a journey that had been filled with happy memories and moments, and starting another that was filled with the possibilities of hurt, despair, and death.

She reached over without thinking and turned on the lamp. Illuminating the fort, her home within a home, she began to gather everything around her.

Chapter Four

The clock showed that it was just past midnight.

The table was no longer set for a missing family, nor beset with personal items that they would find touching should they return to see what she had been up to by herself. Her family wasn't coming back, she finally accepted. Although she still hoped that they would eventually reunite, she knew after reading her uncle's letter that it would not be here.

She had to leave. She would make her way through the city to the docks at its edge, get on a boat, and leave her home to find a new one. The war was coming, and this house would not be safe much longer. Her mother always warned her that a girl by herself would fall victim to the soldiers, and while that certainly could happen to her out there on her own, at least on the road she would have a chance to run away.

No longer caring about tidiness, Nhat ransacked the house looking for things that she would need on the road. Her room looked like a bomb exploded in her dresser after she'd torn it apart looking for clothes that would keep her safe and warm.

Her brother's room now looked similar, his closet thrown open and rummaged through until she discovered his dark blue backpack, which she took without ceremony or sentiment. She'd also been through her father's closet looking for survival supplies. She scavenged a first aid kit, bandages, a combat knife, and a hammer and screwdriver from his small tool kit. More importantly, she found a map of the country, with a big map of her city on the reverse side. Her mother's vanity mirror, once covered in rows of neatly organized jewelry, was now bare. The valuables were now nestled in a plastic bag at the bottom of the backpack

On the kitchen table, she had set out a variety of nonperishable foods: dried meats and fruit, crackers, rice cakes, noodles that she could eat without cooking, powdered milk, and a glass bottle filled with water. She wrapped the pork buns in a hand towel—she would eat these on the first day of her journey. Other items she had plundered included a can opener, a metal cup, and a spoon.

The backpack rested precariously on a chair, stuffed with three changes of clothes, a raincoat, and rain boots. Since it was her brother's, it was bigger and could hold more things. She would look ridiculous carting around a backpack almost as big as herself, but at least she could take more supplies with her. Her own backpack was considerably smaller and bright yellow, so it would carry less and draw more attention to her than her brother's dark blue bag—both things that she considered "no good" for the journey at hand.

She had packed two sets of pants, two black t-shirts, her favorite Woodstock shirt, five pairs of underwear, five pairs of socks, a headband, two hair wraps, and a white scarf from her mother's closet. On her person she wore plain black pants, her third favorite Snoopy t-shirt, and the hiking boots that her father made her wear whenever they went walking in the jungle.

She didn't know much about the real world, but she knew how to generally prepare for outings because of her father. Nhat didn't know how long it would take, but she figured that a couple days' worth of clothing and more food than she could possibly need would get her to the boats. She had money to buy things if she needed, but she didn't want to spend too much. She didn't know how much she would need in the Philippines. The money she would have to use there was a currency that she didn't know. She supplemented the cash with money from her parents' wallets, which she'd found in their room while scavenging the house for supplies. Only now did she realize they hadn't taken them, another indicator that she would not be seeing them again. *At least not here*, she thought hopefully.

With the cash, the clothes, and the other supplies she'd gathered, she at least had a fighting chance.

She didn't have to think much during this process, as her father had drilled all this into his children over and over. What to take, why to take it, how to pack it, having them watch him do it all and help when they could. The whole process came back to her in sequential order as she prepared everything. The only superfluous items found in her bag were his watch, her mom's jewelry, her own stuffed rabbit, and her brother's Swiss Army knife. While the last item had some utility on her journey, it came along more out of sentimental value—something she both needed and, conveniently, wanted.

47

Surveying the table, she decided it was time to pack. First would be her clothes, already in the bag. Her dad always taught her that while the clothes were important, usually you got them out when you were settled down somewhere and ready to change, so they didn't need to be on top. Plus, a soft layer of clothing created a good solid base for the rest of your things.

She took out her raincoat and rain boots, remembering that those needed to go at the top of the bag.

Next came the bag of her mom's jewelry, which she tucked to the side of her clothes so it would be out of the way. She placed her rabbit over it so it would be protected against everything else that would be packed on top.

After that came most of the food, except for the two pork buns and the bottle of water. Those would go in last so she could easily access them and eat that day.

Next, she took the first aid kit, tools, kitchen items, and her father's old combat knife, and arranged them so each could be accessed easily. Finally, she returned her rain boots and raincoat to the bag.

The order had come back to her naturally. With everything packed, all that remained were her day's provisions, her father's watch, her brother's Swiss Army knife, the map, and the documents on the table that she had already separated and sealed shut, following her uncle's instructions.

The watch went into her left pocket and the knife into her right so it could be easily accessed. She put one set of documents in the front pocket of her backpack. The second, which she wrapped in a layer of tape and a sheet from the newspaper, was packed in her raincoat. The third she had wrapped tightly just the way it came because it contained the foreign currency and the tickets. She took care to mimic her uncle's wrapping method exactly. In the end, it was half the thickness of a deck of cards.

She left the last set on the table next to the other three unopened packages—the ones meant for her parents and brother.

Each white packet sat like a tombstone on the table, a stark reminder of a person who, for reasons unknown to her, either forgot her or chose to leave her behind. She wondered which was worse. She wanted to cry, but fear of The Evil down the hall and fear of the war that was coming for her dominated her little heart. The tiny muscle that dictated whether she lived or not didn't know if it could take anything more. It had already been broken on finding that she had been left behind. Now that she had to venture out into the world alone, she had to put that pain at the back of her mind and focus on getting to the docks at the coast. There was nothing else for her here. If there was, they would have come back for her by now.

All the same, she left the packets there for them.

Just in case.

Hopefully they would catch up and she wouldn't have to make the trip to the Philippines or to Hong Kong or to France alone. Maybe they would all be reunited. Maybe they wouldn't. In either case they would need their documents if there was to be any chance of it, so she left them on the table for them to find, next to her fourth copy so they could know she had gone on without them. The way they had gone on without her.

She sighed gently, touching each packet, tracing their names. Turning to the backpack and making sure she had everything, she grabbed the flashlight and went looking for the extra batteries in the kitchen. She found two fresh ones and tucked them into her pocket for quick access before clicking the light off again. Having walked in the darkness the last few days, she had memorized the route to the kitchen and her seat at the table. Once again, she stared at the white packets. She could see them through the darkness in her mind's eye, even if her actual eyes couldn't quite make them out. They stood out like ghosts, each of them watching her silently.

She reached out to touch them once again when she heard it. The growl.

She turned on the flashlight and pointed it towards the door. The growling didn't stop. It continued, low, threatening and audible there in the kitchen. The air grew colder.

Nhat flew off the chair and ran from room to room, turning on every light in the house. Light was the only thing that would save her, light pouring from every room would keep it away from her. The hallway light, the kitchen, the dining area, the living room, all the lamps, the hallway, the bathroom, her room, her brother's, her parents'; every single lamp that could be switched on, was. If electricity ran through it and it illuminated, it was turned on.

49

Back at the table, she made sure everything she needed was in the bag and that she had her dad's watch, brother's knife, and the documents in her pockets. She grabbed the flashlight and, keeping it switched off for now, pointed at the door to her father's office and waited.

The growling had stopped for the moment, but Nhat knew that it was there behind the door, waiting to inflict whatever evil designs it had upon her. Her little heart pounded against her chest as sweat began to drip down her face, the flashlight clutched tightly in one hand and the backpack's straps in the other.

She waited.

The ticking ceased, as if the clock itself held its breath waiting for something to happen. In fact, the whole house fell silent. The dripping faucet froze. The creaking roof sat still. The walls stifled their moaning. The floors stopped settling. Absolute silence prevailed, as the house itself waited to see whether the horror confined to the office would be unleashed upon its last remaining resident.

Nhat stood facing the door, the fluorescence of her house doing little to comfort her. The Evil would be deterred by light, this she somehow knew, but would the whole house of hers and the flashlight she held in her hand be enough?

Time had a funny way of showing itself in moments of distress and terror. How long had she been standing there, waiting for something to happen? A minute? A second? Five hours? Five days?

Light bore into her skin the way it hadn't in three days. She had grown accustomed to living in the shadows and in darkness. Her skin tingled from the light of artificial suns that she had formerly banished for her own safety.

Relaxing her body, she felt her muscles loosen around the flashlight and backpack. She finally sighed, knowing that the lights had worked and that The Evil –

WHAM.

The door shook with thunderous force, rocking its frame and sending vibrations through the wall and floor.

Nhat jumped back against the table in absolute horror. The fruit bowl, which was now empty as she had packed the food in her backpack, rattled on the table. Whether it was on account of her jumping into it or from the Evil banging on the door, she did not know.

50

Not even a second passed before the door shook once again, attacked by the thing that had taken over her father's office and manifested into the terror that Nhat now faced on her own.

WHAM.

The kitchen light went out. She looked over, terror in her eyes, wanting to believe that it had been a coincidence.

WHAM.

The light in the hallway leading to the bedrooms went out. Maybe another coincidence?

WHAM.

The bedroom lights went out.

WHAM.

Then the living room lights.

WHAM.

The lamps. One by one, they all went out. Only the kitchen light and hallway light by the front door remained.

WHAM.

The kitchen light went out.

WHAM.

The light by the door flickered, but was not extinguished.

Nhat did not wait any longer. She grabbed the backpack, clicked the flashlight on, and crept towards the front door. Keeping a watchful eye on her father's office while glancing back to make sure the last remaining light in the house stayed on, she inched closer to her only exit, step by step.

WHAM.

The sound made her jump, and finally she ran to the front door, fumbling with its locks when the last light in her home went out.

Absolute darkness was terrifying in and of itself. When you know for certain that something evil is lurking within it, it takes on new dimensions of horror that only the human mind can imagine. Nhat could not comprehend this level of fear, of desperation, of pure terror. The only thing she could do was freeze when, as she fumbled with the locks at her front door, absolute darkness descended upon her and The Evil knocking at her father's office door was finally released.

She turned around slowly when the final forceful slam released the door from its hinges. The same ice-cold winter air that she had felt inside the office rushed out and filled the entire house, the hair on her arms

51

prickling up in response. The terror that was growing in her heart crystallized and spread up to her throat. She couldn't have cried out if she wanted to, and in the silent darkness, she clutched at her flashlight and watched the cold white clouds escape her tiny mouth.

Her back against the door, she felt the backpack pressing against the bottom of her legs. She had hitched up the straps as far as they would go, but still felt the backpack was too large. Reaching behind her, she struggled with the locks again, eyes fixed ahead at where the office door should be. The last lock was the stiff deadbolt, and her little fingers had trouble finding the strength to open it. She dared not avert her gaze from the office door, however, where she knew The Evil was lurking. Like a wild animal, she knew that turning her back to it would surely invite it to attack.

The deadbolt would not budge. Even under normal circumstances it had always been difficult for her to manage. There in the dark, behind her back with one hand, it would almost be impossible. She would have to turn and face it if she intended to open it and break free from whatever evil was now consuming all the light and warmth within the house. Her legs glued to the floor, she was still fumbling with the lock when she heard the familiar growl out in the hall.

In the confined space of the office, the growl had been a menacing, overwhelming sound, one that had almost driven her right out through the sheer force of its imposing presence. In the hall, it was sinister, focused, and directed straight at her.

Nhat's little body began to shake at what she now knew to be an open threat. Her brain commanded her hand to turn on the flashlight, but her body remained unresponsive in the presence of pure evil.

The growl increased in volume. It was getting closer. She heard clicking on the tile floor. She couldn't see anything but imagined talons or claws rapping on the floor, long fanglike nails that clicked as it walked towards her.

Images of various monsters and demons flashed across her mind as she tried to figure out what could be growling at her and clicking on the floor as it crept. Was it a huge wolf maybe, or a dinosaur-like lizard with a long tongue that would choke her before it ate her? Had a harpy, a witch with the wings and legs of a vicious bird, come to spirit her away? She pictured the wolf grabbing her with its large mouth and furiously ripping her apart, the lizard holding her down with its talons and ripping out her stomach while she was still alive, the harpy lifting her into the air and ripping her limb from limb, her body parts falling to the ground like tree limbs in a monsoon.

In her mind's terrified eye, she saw all three creatures descend upon her, each taking their turn at eating her, killing her, mutilating her body here in her home where she waited dutifully for her family. Was it The Evil that killed them? Did they discover it and run away without her because they were so afraid? All these scenarios and questions ran through her mind, broken only by what she saw in the darkest shadow of her once happy home.

The growling had stopped. She sensed that The Evil was still by the office door, waiting to pounce on her and strike. In the few seconds of silence, she perceived only the beating of her own heart and the evil desires emanating from the darkness. As she was about to move again for the lock, two yellow orbs appeared before her. It took only a moment to realize that these were the creature's eyes. They were almond shaped, devoid of any sort of humanity or goodwill. The bright, sickly yellow exuded malice with an intensity that would consume her and all that was good in the world. The eyes were the size of volleyballs, which led her to draw terrible conclusions about the size of the beast itself. The eyes were brilliant and focused, yet cast no light on anything around them, relegated only to the slanted orbs themselves. Tiny black pupils the size of limes rested in their centers. The Evil had a form and a face and eyes, and from the darkness in her home, it stared directly into her soul.

Nhat let out a piercing scream. The Evil recoiled, taken aback by the shrill noise, its eyes narrowing as it backed up slightly. She turned around and, with a strength she had never felt before, threw open the dead bolt, flung open the door, and stole into the night like a cat, slamming the door behind her.

53

Chapter Five

Nhat never thought about running. Most of the time she just did it. Rarely in her life had she been told to run for a purpose. Most of the time it was for play, to get somewhere fast, to expel the pent-up energy that comes with just being a child. She had only ever been *told* to run for games, running away from the angry stray dog, or when being tormented by her brother, but never before had she run for fear of her life. Tag? Sure. Chasing the boy she liked in a circle? Absolutely. From the menace that was her brother with a spider on a stick? More than she cared to remember. From an oppressing evil that wanted to devour her? Never before.

In the dark streets of the city, she ran for her life. Away from her family home. Away from everything she knew. Away from the two deathly evil eyes of a creature she could not see.

She felt it behind her. Five seconds out of the door she could feel the cold licking at her feet. The streets were empty. The lights were off, both because of the need to conserve electricity and to prevent enemy soldiers from spotting the town and attacking it from a distance. She didn't know these things directly; she had only heard her mother and father talking about them. That's why the shades at home were always drawn closed and only the low lamps were used in the living room.

A thought flashed through her mind that made her stomach churn: *Did I alert the enemy by turning on all the lights at home?* But the idea left her head just as quickly as it had come, as death was fast at her feet.

The flurry of her steps echoed through the night, slamming on the dry pavement that was cracking at the edges. Her short, shallow breathing dominated her ears as she sprinted down the street she used to take when walking to school.

She wanted to think of her brother, who would walk this street with her before joining up with his friends at the intersection, but there was no time. The intersection was coming up and she had to remember very quickly which way the big part of the city was. She needed to get to

54

the big part of the city to get to the dirty part of the city, which would then take her to the pretty part of the city where the big boats were.

Nhat looked behind her and saw the yellow eyes in the distance. It was following her.

She remembered that going to the left meant going to school, going straight meant going further into the neighborhood, and going right was something they only did when they went somewhere as a family on their bikes. Usually to somewhere nice—a park, the restaurant her parents loved, or to run some important errand. She wasn't going to school or to her friend's house, so she went right.

Running full speed ahead, she veered off to the left before looping around to the right. She couldn't make a sharp turn at that speed and she didn't want to fall, knowing that The Evil was still in pursuit. She didn't know what would happen if it caught up to her. She could be eaten alive, torn apart, any number of other indescribable things. Whatever The Evil would do to her, she didn't want to experience it.

She veered to the right, little legs pumping, heart threatening to escape her chest, cold sweat running down her forehead, and raced into the dark street relying on what little guidance her memory could give her.

A crash thundered behind her. She turned back and saw the thing that had been chasing her was the size of half a bus. She saw the yellow eyes blinking in the dark before turning to her. The Evil was larger than she imagined and moved on four legs, that much she could see, and somehow she had tricked it into thinking she was going the other way. She had gained a couple seconds after it crashed and fell, but now she knew she had angered it.

She ran faster.

The darkness of the street encroached upon her. She saw little glimpses of lights here and there, but they were mere pinpricks accentuating the darkness of the dead of night and the fear that dominated her little heart.

Nhat wanted to cry out for help, but she didn't dare. The danger lurking in the darkness was both from people that she didn't know and from The Evil that was now again chasing her, angry that she had tricked it, and she could not risk giving away her presence to either.

Tears streamed from her eyes but she dared not cry out or try to wipe them away. The only thing to do was run until she could escape The

Evil or find a place to hide. If it was even possible to hide from such a thing.

As the tears continued to well up and pour from her eyes, she noticed the stars and how brightly they shone in the night sky. She focused on them and their light as she ran; along with the meager illumination the moon offered, it was all she had to guide her.

She looked around desperately, trying to see if there was a street to veer off to or a place to hide in the dark. A refuge where she could turn on the flashlight and protect herself against the darkness that was behind and all around her.

She felt her legs going numb, and knew that they were running out of steam. She became very aware of how tired she was and felt her body begin to slow down despite her screaming at her legs internally to keep going.

The stars grew brighter for her, urging her to go on.

Her little neck turned as far as it could without sacrificing more of her already decreasing speed. The Evil was still in pursuit, its eyes the size of tennis balls in the distance but growing slightly larger every second.

It was catching up to her.

There was nothing for Nhat to do but run. She forward once again, keeping her eyes on the stars to focus. They grew bright, hanging in the sky as beacons, lighting the way in the dark by giving her a focal point. If she could keep her eyes on the stars she could keep going and hopefully find a way to escape the monster behind her.

Growling noises again reached her ear. The Evil was getting closer. She shut her eyes so she wouldn't be tempted to turn again and look, and ran faster despite her legs burning in protest as her lungs wheezed angrily. She ran blind, her eyes shut, willing her body to do everything it could to keep going.

Opening her eyes again, she looked to the stars, which now burned with magnificence. Like The Evil's eyes, they were the size of tennis balls now and ever increasing. She was certain she wasn't imagining it now; to her shock and awe, the stars were getting brighter.

Nhat quickly looked to her right and left and at the street ahead; she could see the faint light increasing. A white shine had appeared as the stars exuded light that now allowed her to see her surroundings. She saw the outlines of houses and buildings, made out the sign of a general store that she rode by on her bike with her family, and the irregularities of the street.

She looked to the stars again, the once tennis ball sized objects had now reached the size of melons. They were not only getting closer, but they looked as if they were coming to her.

Finally, her legs gave out underneath her and Nhat slammed into the street, tumbling forward like a top-heavy rag doll, her legs splaying over her head she rolled. She felt her face and arms scrape against the road as they slid across the uneven pavement and patches of dirt.

She lay there, the dirt from the ground sticking to her face and fresh wounds, breathing heavily, waiting for The Evil to pounce upon her and do whatever it was going to do. Eyes clenched shut, she waited for what was to be her end.

The end, however, didn't come. Through her closed eyes she felt the cold that The Evil had brought with it but also a strange new warmth. Her eyelids began to glow, as if someone were shining a light in her face.

Nhat opened her eyes to see the street totally illuminated, as if someone had turned on a streetlamp that shone light in every direction. There were no shadows, and though the light could not compare to the sun, it shone brightly enough to sneak into every nook and cranny of the surrounding buildings.

Eyes wide open, Nhat sat up and looked behind her. There she saw The Evil for what it was; a horrible demon waiting at a distance, with bright yellow eyes that peered at her hungrily as if it deciding whether to eat her slowly or tear her apart first.

The intensity of the light around Nhat was increasing still, forcing The Evil backward. Even though it wasn't directly in the light, she could still see *it*.

The mass that looked like a large wolf's body still held the general shape, but in the dim light of whatever was illuminating the area, she could see that it most decidedly was not a wolf. In fact, she didn't know what it was. The Evil stood on four legs like a dog, but it had no fur. Its pale skin had a white sheen in the light, with a pattern that was hard to describe. When Nhat thought she could see it, it was different, and when she thought she finally had it, it changed again. The third time it happened, she squinted her eyes and stared more closely. The skin was not patterned—it was moving. The size of the beast was scary enough on its own; the sight

57

of its skin crawling across the surface of its body gave way to a new kind of terror. Focusing on the side of the beast, she saw that what looked like maggots and worms crawling all over The Evil. She looked below it but didn't see anything on the ground. These maggots and worms were stuck to it, constantly moving.

She whimpered, realizing that what she thought was skin might not even be skin at all.

The Evil heard this, snarled, and came forward into the light slightly before recoiling again as it grew brighter still.

Nhat's heart and mind were in danger of shutting down. It was here when she saw the creature move that she understood the skin wasn't moving, but rather that The Evil was made up of these worms and maggots. When it moved its two front legs the claws that dug into the ground seemed to disappear and reappear back on the surface. Its body lengthened into the darkness and the old legs disappeared, looking more now like a large serpent. The Evil seemed simultaneously ready to pounce on Nhat and recoil into the darkness like the snake that it was.

Nhat closed her eyes and waited for the attack, but it never came. She opened them to see that the light had grown brighter and that The Evil had retreated further to avoid it. She met its bright yellow gaze and examined its face.

Like the rest of The Evil's body, its face was made up of pale worms and maggots. They were grey, yellow, and light pink, a combination of colors that somehow made her feel sick and dizzy. Its face was sick and hungry, eager to kill. Its bald features made it look like a dog that had been burned alive and was still breathing, waiting for its master to pet it. The ear-like protrusions were jagged, the area around its eyes squirmed like exposed muscle, and its mouth was an expanse of gums without lips. Drool fell freely to the floor, creating pools of a wretched liquid that gave off an equally vile stench.

It changed shape again, back into the form of a large wolf or dog. This was the shape The Evil had chosen. This was what it wanted to be. Nhat recoiled in fear because she was afraid of dogs, and she knew that The Evil knew this too. The Evil could be whatever it wanted to be. It wanted to be this for her.

It bared its teeth at Nhat, a lipless smile threatening violence.

Nhat cried out, not because of the show of hostility, but because of the teeth themselves.

Where she was expecting sharp fangs and rows of razor-sharp spikes, she instead saw a perfect line of human teeth. White, straight, the spitting image of perfection, there, grinding themselves, waiting to tear into her little body.

All the same, The Evil kept its distance. The light seemed to stabilize, and it prevented the creature from moving any closer.

While still terrified, Nhat's heartbeat calmed a bit after her mad sprint and she was able to control her breathing again. She sat in the pool of light, waiting for it to attack until she realized that it wouldn't.

"You're afraid of it," she said out loud. Not talking to The Evil, itself, but simply stating that she knew it was afraid of the light and that it used the darkness to chase her. "You're afraid of light," she thought back to the flashlight and realized that she was no longer holding it. She looked around and saw it a few feet ahead of her. She got up, wincing in pain, and walked towards it.

The Evil growled behind her again, baring its perfect human teeth. Nhat paid it no mind and picked up the flashlight. She flicked it on, turned and shone it directly in The Evil's face.

The Evil let out a roar, jumping back, its legs disappearing and reforming in the air as it landed in the complete darkness. Its body hidden by the shadows, all Nhat could see were its yellow eyes boring hatefully into her own.

"Don't toy with it," she heard a voice say. It was soft, gentle, and all around her. Nhat turned quickly and shone the flashlight everywhere, even though the soft white light illuminated everything around her. The voice sounded so close, as if it had whispered into her ear.

"What you are saying is correct; it does not like the light. But do not mistake its prudence for a lack of want. If you mock it, it *will* hurt itself to destroy you."

Nhat looked around fervently, trying to identify the source of the voice.

"Look above you," it said softly, once again as if whispering in her ear. The voice brought her peace, the light warmth, despite The Evil that was waiting in the shadows to harm her. She lowered the light, allowing herself to relax slightly, and looked up.

Where the stars once twinkled, a singular light had taken their place. It was the size of a manhole cover, large but no bigger than Nhat herself. She tilted her head to the side, both in awe and confusion at the light floating in front of her.

"What are you?" she asked, naturally curious. She had already registered The Evil in her mind, it took little effort to accept this peaceful entity as fact.

"We are the light."

"The light?"

"That's right Nhat. We're here to protect you."

"Protect me?"

"That's right."

"Protect me from The Evil?" Nhat asked.

"You are correct, though we call it something else. You can keep calling it 'The Evil'."

"What do you call it?"

A growl came from behind her. Nhat turned and saw that The Evil had once again made itself known at the light's edge.

It stood on all fours like a wolf ready to strike. Its back was arched, neck lowered, legs in a punching strike, and teeth bared. The human teeth that were smiling at her now, while its wild yellow eyes divulged its thirst for her blood.

"It will strike very soon," the light said to her. "Are you able to run?"

Nhat looked at the light in both fear and confusion.

"Do not worry child, we will guide you. Are you able to?"

Nhat looked down at herself, she checked her scrapes and cuts, her pockets, and made sure she still had the backpack and all its contents. Everything was in order. She looked at the light and nodded.

"Good. The Evil knows what I am going to do because we've fought before. I will break off a small piece of myself. You follow that piece and leave my bigger self to deal with the creature. Understand?"

Nhat wasn't entirely sure what was happening, but she trusted the light implicitly the same way she naturally feared The Evil. She looked up and nodded.

"Good. Follow The Fox."

60

The light pulsed, and a tiny fox leapt out of the ball. The ball itself broke into several medium sized orbs and jetted towards The Evil like bullets from a gun.

Nhat ran, following The Fox down the street. Its body was silver, as if carved from the full moon, and it ran deftly down the street guiding Nhat to safety.

She had never seen a fox in real life before, much less seen one running down the street. For all she knew this white fox could have been a real animal that glowed like a star, and not a spectral light that was leading her to safety.

The Fox left a trail of light, darting down the road, taking Nhat on a twisting, turning route. Sometimes she would lose sight of it, only to turn the corner and see it there, body straight, tail down, ears perked up to the sky, waiting for her and then darting off again.

The two ran for what felt like an eternity. The Fox would lead her for long stretches straight down one street before taking a series of what seemed to her like random twists and turns down alleys and staircases. She heard water and with the light cast by The Fox she saw that they were passing by a small canal that she and her brother once spent an afternoon throwing rocks into. She tried to recreate the image in her head, but she was running so much she could barely do anything but keep up with The Fox.

They ran far longer than she had sprinted by herself before. This time, however, the pace was controlled, her breathing was level, and even though her legs were begging for her to stop, she was able to keep going and follow the silver creature.

When she felt she could no longer go on, when she was tempted to call out for a break, The Fox stopped, sat on its haunches and waited while she caught her breath.

Hands on her knees, she hunched over and gulped down air, her lungs working overtime to oxygenate every ounce of blood that pumped through her legs and arms. She felt it more in her legs, but her arms were sorer than she realized from holding the backpack straps. The bag kept smacking her on the back, so the only thing to do was to hold the straps down in order to lift the bag. It worked in that her back wasn't sore from being slapped with her cargo, but now her little arms were weary.

Standing there in the deep dark night, hunched over, gasping for breath, she felt the light emanating from The Fox and for the first time looked up to get a good look at it. She had kept her eyes on it while they were running, but here in the middle of the dark street that she didn't know, she could finally *see* it.

The Fox itself was magnificently beautiful. It looked like a real fox, its pointy ears erect, its sharp snout held high in the air, and its soft white fur glowed with its own radiated light. She understood that it wasn't an actual fox but the light taking the form of one.

"I am neither animal nor being," The Fox said, revealing that it understood her look. "I simply am."

Nhat gasped. "I don't understand that." She didn't. It looked like an animal, behaved like one, but she also knew it wasn't one. She just didn't know what it had meant by "I simply am."

The Fox didn't care to explain, it simply sat and waited for her to rest.

Time passed, and with each breath she grew calmer, until she remembered why she had been running and panicked. She turned around in a flurry, switching on the flashlight that she had been clutching this entire time.

"It won't be after you again this evening," The Fox said soothingly. "It doesn't know where you are, and for now you are safe."

"For now?" She turned around and shone the light on The Fox.

"It knows you, Nhat. It will never stop hunting you." The Fox tilted its head. "You can turn that off now."

Nhat turned off the light but still glanced behind her. Was The Fox right? Was it really hunting her?

"It won't stop until you are far away from here." The Fox said, again, being privy to her thoughts.

"How far?" she asked, feeling the packet burn in her pocket. The plan radiated through her mind, her escape weighing heavily on hear heart.

"Away from this place." The Fox turned its head away from her and down into the darkness that neither could see into. "Out of the city, past the sand, into the water, and onto foreign shores." The Fox turned to look at her once again, waiting for her to reply. She never did. In her mind, that would mean accepting what she knew she had to do.

"Will I ever see them again?"

The Fox tilted its head at her before giving it a small shake.

"That's not for me to say. I only know that I am here to guide you away from this place and The Evil that stalks you."

Nhat stood, her legs aching, her arms beginning to tremble. The physical exertion matched by the weighty realization that she would probably never see her family again, all against the backdrop of the horror behind her and the magic of the light radiating off The Fox in front of her.

"What do I do?" she asked The Fox, more a plea for help than asking for instructions.

"For now," The Fox nodded towards a nearby door, "hide."

Nhat looked where it had motioned, a plain door in a building that she did not recognize.

"In there?" she asked.

The Fox nodded. "You will be safe there for tonight. It will take a long time for The Evil to find you, but he will." The Fox gazed directly into her eyes, its brightness both comforting her and assuring her of the awful truth it was telling her. "You must move only during the day in order to escape The Evil, but you will not make it to your boat in time without traveling at night as well." The Fox looked as though it sighed, but she didn't hear it.

"But won't it get me if I go out at night?"

"Yes," The Fox nodded, "which is why we will help you. However, we can only do so much each night." The Fox settled down, like a real fox laying down to sleep. "For now, you must rest and hide, and we must return to the sky to rest as well." The Fox laid its head down. "Go into the building, it's empty. Sleep with your flashlight close by and leave at the break of dawn. Travel until the sun goes down and then run. When The Evil finds you again—because it will—so will we."

Before Nhat could say anything, The Fox faded away. She sat once again in darkness with only the moon as a guide. She looked at the door in the dark, took a small breath, and weakly walked into the building.

The door shut on the night, shut on her old life, shut on her childhood, shut on seeing her family ever again, and shut on The Evil prowling the streets guttling her name.

Chapter Six

Dawn crept like a thief in the night. Nhat had hardly slept, and when she did it was filled with nightmares of the skinless thing that chased her tearing her mother, father and brother apart. She watched in her dreams as its mass of flesh, the crawling things that made up its body, smiled at her as it sank its human teeth into her family. Her mother howled out, her father screamed in pain, and her brother called to her for help. The yellow eyes of The Evil bored into her as blood rushed from its mouth and the crunch of bones filled her ears. Always smiling, always grinning as it formed long limbs to support itself. One arm bent, holding itself up, as the other lay at rest on its hunched leg, snacking on her family like fruit bought from the market.

She would wake up crying, wanting to call out for her mother, but instead whimpered in the dark and abandoned office to which The Fox had led her. She hid underneath a desk, using her pack as a pillow, her flashlight as her weapon, and her raincoat as a blanket. It was the worst thing she'd had to do so far. Shivering, she would clutch the flashlight to her chest, watching the door to make sure The Evil didn't discover her. She pictured it bursting through the door, scanning the room with its horrible yellow eyes and smiling with its human teeth when it found her and crept over to her, its wet body making no sound as it closed in on her, sucking up her fear. Eventually exhaustion would take her, only for another nightmare to wake her up and repeat the process until she finally saw hints of light entering the abandoned office building.

Her body ached all over. The previous night had demanded everything from her. Still, The Fox told her to leave at dawn, and she wasn't about to ignore it after it had saved her from The Evil. Well, delayed it, at least.

It won't stop it said, the words echoing in her mind as she crawled out from underneath the desk and stretched her limbs.

She scratched at her head, tussling her long black hair, shaking it for any dirt or debris that might have stayed in there from when she fell.

64

Satisfied that nothing was there, she stood and examined her surroundings. Having only used her flashlight in quick bursts, she didn't get a good look at the place last night. She was still worried about being found out by other people if she used the flashlight too much. Though a demon hunted her while she tried to sleep, other people were still very much a danger to her.

The office was simply furnished; there were desks, a water cooler, and several filing cabinets. The desks were devoid of anything that showed people worked there. She had chosen the desk farthest away from the door, figuring it was the safest one.

Now fully awake, she began to feel her body ask for the things that she had denied it amidst yesterday night's chaos. She walked over to the water cooler, but it was empty. Nhat huffed and walked back to the desk where she slept and pulled out her bag. She took the bottle of water out and took a sip. She knew better than to drink too much, she didn't know where her next drink would come from.

Her stomach growled. The water hit an empty spot and her body once again reminded her of the energy she exerted and the fact that it was morning and time for food. She set the bottle down on the ground, crouched next to the pack and pulled out one of the two pork buns. These would be eaten today, as they would not be good tomorrow.

She gently unwrapped it and sat down, ignoring the pain in her legs and back. She crossed her legs and put the bun in front of her. Palms together, she said a prayer thanking God for her food and took another small sip of water before digging into the white bao that her mother had made before she disappeared with the rest of the family.

As Nhat chewed, she asked out loud. "Did they disappear, or did they leave me?" The question lingered in her mind as she quietly ate her food. The sweet meat was not as cold as it would have been straight out of the refrigerator, but the morning air didn't allow it to completely warm up. Cold baos were one of Nhat's favorite things. Here on the floor, her limbs aching, the sweet and tender meat that filled the soft dough lifted her spirits a bit. For a fleeting moment she ate and was again a little girl enjoying a little girl's favorite thing. Just for a moment.

The next moment was spent in contemplation once again. "Did they disappear, or did they leave me?" The question would not leave her alone. It stayed in the recesses and the forefront of her mind, like two independent beings waiting for an answer she couldn't give. One, waiting at the fore of her mind, wanted the answer now. The other, digging in the back of her subconscious, looked at anything it could find as some clue. An obscure memory, some old fact, a feeling, anything that it could use to formulate *some* kind of answer. Which is all she wanted. Something that could tell her what happened to her family or where they had gone and why.

"Maybe they are The Evil," she said out loud, her mouth full of the sweet and salty pork bun her mother had made not too long ago. She swallowed and looked down at the half-eaten treat. "Maybe they are the monster," she added, her voice tinged with sorrow and despair. She felt tears well up again, but she wiped them away and forced herself to eat. Instead of dwelling on that nasty possibility, she chose to focus on the bao's sweet filling, savoring every morsel leading up to that swig of cool water that would fill her mouth, flushing out any lingering flavor and leaving her cool and refreshed like a nice spring day.

Day. She looked to the window and, while she couldn't see the sun itself, she saw the orange and pink glow peeking over the horizon.

Nhat had hardly ever seen the sunrise; this was something she was not usually up for, and when she was her father wanted to be left alone or her mother was fussing at her to help with the morning preparations.

Standing up, she set the unfinished bao on its wrapper to protect it from the dust on the floor. Nhat felt pain in her body again. While it wasn't severe or stabbing as it had been the night before, it was enough to remind her that she was in danger and that evil things, human and otherwise, were chasing her.

Just under four feet tall, she stood on her toes to look out the window. She rested her arms on the sill and let her feet dangle just a little bit. Her arms weren't too sore to support her, and her legs were thankful for the stretch they got while hanging there.

A few strands of her black her fell over her face. Nhat left them there as she lay her head on her arms, watching the sky being washed over with ever brightening hues of cream pink, orange, and white.

Smiling wasn't something she had done much in the last few days, but a smile pulled at the corners of her mouth as she watched the pink spreading in the sky. It was one of her favorite colors. Not because she was a girl, but because it reminded her of happier times. Of strawberries. Of flowers. Of the ice cream her brother shared with her. Of her father's

66

cheeks whenever she kissed him on the face. Of her mother's heart when she lay her head on it and fell asleep listening to the gentle rhythms of her mother's love. It was just a color, but it filled her heart with so much.

However, just as her life had changed, so too did the color of the sky.

With the coming of the sun, the sky went from a creamsicle orange and pink with touches of white, to a blood red. The sun had finally crested and took all the gentleness of dawn and replaced with it with the coming doom of war.

The sky had turned into blood. So too, did Nhat's thoughts.

She let her feet touch down, went back to her seat on the floor, and ate the rest of her bao, thinking about The Evil lurking in the shadows and the war marching towards her and the rest of the city.

She ate quickly, remembering how her father had always rushed her brother to finish eating. There on the ground, she shoved bits of bao and sweet red pork into her mouth, mimicking her brother's frenzied actions. Actions that lived only in her memory.

I   t was much more difficult to put the notion of quickly eating into practice than it was visualizing it, and Nhat had to slow down. She almost choked on one of the bigger bits of meat and had to take an unscheduled sip of water to stop herself from coughing. She ate the rest of the bao with urgency, but took her time to chew correctly so as to avoid chocking to death in the abandoned offices. The thought almost made her chuckle. It would be silly for her to die that way with a demon stalking her every step and a war raging around her

The war had changed the way her family lived forever, and it was the reason she was out in the city like this, in the open, trying to escape. She was also certain, that the war had brought down The Evil upon her somehow. Something in this city was going bad, and it caused The Evil to form in her house. With all the bad that had been going on in her home— her father hitting her mother, their mother always being so stingy with the food, her brother acting out more and more, and she, neglected among it all—it was no wonder that The Evil had chosen her father's office to come and hide and wait for her.

"Maybe it ate everyone," she finally said out loud, holding the last piece of bao in her hand, the red glaze from the meat staining the white dough and reminding her of all the horrible ways that The Evil could kill

67

her. Wanting to set it down, she hesitated and ate it regardless, hearing her mother's stern words that there was a war going on and she should feel grateful that they had meat to eat. The sweet meat turned bitter in her mouth, the soft bun rough as it passed half-masticated down her throat, the water stale as she washed the taste of death out of her mouth.

She stood, knowing she couldn't stay there much longer. The Fox warned her that she needed to keep moving. With the mass of flesh and perfect teeth chasing her, she intended to get as far away from it as she could today.

Packing her things, she gazed out the window and saw that the sun had fully come up. It was a beautiful day outside. One where she could see herself outside playing with her friends or walking with her brother to the park on some adventure that he had planned but didn't tell her about. She was hit with a wave of nostalgia for a time that was not too long ago. She didn't even know the word she wanted to use was "nostalgia," she just felt that ache in her heart for happier times.

"Be sad and walk," she said, and forced herself to pack the few things she took out of her pack. She placed the remaining bao on top of her packed items, knowing that today would be the last day she would be able to eat it. The meat wasn't too appealing after imagining The Evil devouring her family, but she had only so much food and she knew that she couldn't waste it. The journey she was going to take would be long and she didn't know when or where her next meal would come from. If she made it, that is.

There was an urge to stop and take stock of the place that she had called home that night, a feeling that wanted her to give some importance to the place and pay respects to it. Instead, Nhat resisted the sentimentality that she had always carried with her and pushed the door open, letting in the morning air.

The office had been stuffy and smelled of old paper. The morning air reached Nhat's tiny nose and caused it to crinkle at the mix of the fresh and the decaying. She closed her eyes and took a deep breath, wanting to take in the new air. It was then she realized that it wasn't just the office that smelled that way, there was a tint in the air of something dying. The smell reminded her of last night, of the smell of decay that had accompanied The Evil.

Shadows lingered between the buildings where the sun had yet to reach. In the cool morning shade, she stood and shivered, reminded of the terror that she had yet to escape from. Safety lay in the light of day, so for now, she was OK. In several hours she wouldn't be. There was no time to be afraid or enjoy the small things. She had to go.

***

The city was half deserted. Taking tiny cautious steps, Nhat ventured out onto the street. In the distance she saw people walking and riding their bikes on streets that crossed the one she was on, but she didn't hear the normal hustle and bustle of the city. The roar of cars and bikes, honking at anything and everything, the loud chatter of people— everything Nhat knew about what a city sounded and looked like was absent. She didn't have to wonder why; she knew it was because of the war. She just didn't know how terribly it had truly affected everything.

Creeping onward, she gazed upon her surroundings, half in awe at the city and in the fact that she was out here venturing through it all alone.

Perhaps even just a few moments earlier that would have brought her to tears, but this lovely revelation instead sparked her own bravery, and gradually she began to walk faster, grip the straps of her brother's backpack tighter, and walk with her head held on high.

She crossed a street, the still-rising sun casting its light gently upon her face. Nhat smiled and closed her eyes as she crossed, feeling its warmth. Passing between the rows of buildings again, she was met with the cold of the night that lingered in the shade. In a half hour, that too would be gone. Even though she wanted the sun more, she thought she should enjoy the cool air while she could before the heat and humidity suffocated her and everyone else in this city. The days were long but the humidity and heat made them feel even longer.

For a moment Nhat felt a sense of peace, something she had not felt for quite some time. Though it had only been a few days since her ordeal began, it felt to her like an eternity. Time moves so slowly in the mind of a child, ever yearning for that next birthday, holiday, or other special occasion promised by their loved ones. They long for adulthood, lamenting how long it would take to get there. All that Nhat longed for now, however, were her parents and brother. The four days that she had

69

been without them were lifetimes within a lifetime for her. Here in the city, walking in the cool shade with the sun spreading its life around her, she felt a tiny dose of that small comfort she had been waiting for and held onto it. Just like the shade, it would soon evaporate, and she would be faced again with the reality of her situation and the heartache that came with it.

Her feet gently pattered against the concrete sidewalk. Taking a glance around, she wondered if anyone would say anything or if she would get in trouble for walking in the street. Or worse, get hit by a car.

But there was no one around, and her mother wasn't here to scold her for running to and from the other side of the street, using the wide expanse as her own personal playground. Still, she looked around cautiously, hesitating from an ingrained fear.

Stopping, she turned and looked up and down the street. She saw a slow but steady crawl of cars, motorcycles, mopeds, and bicycles, but none turned. Behind her and in front of her, the street remained untouched by oncoming traffic.

Forgetting for a moment that her family had abandoned her. Forgetting for a moment that a war was coming. Forgetting for a moment that a demon was chasing her down. Nhat relaxed her shoulders and knees, walked into the middle of the street, and played.

She ran to each side of the street, her arms splayed out like an airplane. She hopped over cracks and balanced herself on the curb as she took steps to avoid the bottomless pit that the street represented. She imagined boxes with numbers on the ground and hopscotched for a few moments. She skipped in large circles, keeping an eye out for cars and bikes that never came. She found a large stick in the gutter and immediately brandished it; she was a pirate on the seven seas and a swordfighter from the stories her father told her. Imaginary foes left and right fell to Nhat's prowess as she fought through endless amounts of enemies shouting her name. The stick then turned into a microphone and, skipping to an imaginary beat, Nhat sang to the crowd of adoring fans cheering her on.

Giggling, she smiled ear to ear and for a small moment acted her age. She didn't know it right then and there, but this would be the last time she would.

70

Chapter Seven

She had been a valiant warrior about to save the prince from a mighty giant when the crash of a breaking window in the distance brought her back to reality. She stopped, listening for anything that might sound like a war, but all she heard was two grownups arguing. It reminded her of her parents at first, but in the end it was just two people arguing over who was at fault for the broken window.

Nhat looked around. The street was still empty but the crash of breaking glass had made her nervous and she quickly returned to the sidewalk. Play time was over and now she returned to a reality where things crashed and broke and she had to avoid things that could crash and break around her.

She continued walking and wondered what she would do when she got to the cross street. Nhat knew that the coast was to the east. Eventually she would have to turn toward where the sun was rising and head that way. After going in the correct general direction she would have to find two big streets that crossed each other, check the map to find out where she was, and plot a path from there out of the city.

"That's going to be hard" she said out loud. Her father had tried to teach her maps in the past, but she always resisted it. The lines and symbols intimidated her. While she did retain some of the information, she always relied on her big brother to guide them when their father sent them off to find their own way. It sounds cruel to explain it in such a way, but their father was never too far from them, watching, nodding in approval when they'd take the correct turn or point out a landmark they'd found.

Nhat looked around to see if her family was watching her, still hoping this was all some kind of test, but all she saw was a bare street and, in her mind's eye, the grinning set of disturbingly perfect teeth that wanted to tear her apart.

She shuddered. The Evil had made an appearance in her imagination when all she wanted to do was forget it. Instead it followed her as if it were there, waiting for her, watching her, hungry for her flesh.

71

Nhat stopped, shook her head, and focused on her family until the evil smile was gone and all she could see were the faces of those she loved.

The cross street she was walking toward loomed closer with each cautious step. In a moment she would be among other people for the first time without her family to look out for her. This was different from school, where she had her brother and friends and the teachers that took care of her. Here, she had no one. Her heart thumped faster, feeling like it would climb into her throat if it could. Her breathing became erratic. Her hands, tightly clutching the backpack straps, started to sweat. Her blinking rapidly increased. She was about to be among city people. People worried and braced for war. People who act in unpredictable, unfamiliar ways. People who might be willing to hurt her.

She stopped.

She couldn't move. She was moments away from stepping out onto the street with other people and she was afraid. She had spent the last few days living alone, had spent the previous night running away from a demon and sleeping in an abandoned building that a fox told her was safe, yet here she stood: immobilized by the prospect of a busy street. The clatter of the bike chains, the roar of the motorbikes, and the hum of passing cars all mixed with the subtle droning of people going about their business. It all gave her pause, but before her feet could freeze completely something caught her eye.

It was a white butterfly.

Her fear began to melt away as the butterfly flew soft circles around her. There in the middle of the street it mystified her. She had only seen them at her home in her mother's garden and at school around the trees, never here in the city. The scene was truly magical to her. It was small, its bright white wings clearly defined against the grey of the city, as if colored by starlight. The body, too, stood out; it was so bright it was almost silver. She stood in awe of the beautiful, winged insect as it fluttered in front of her, inviting her to touch it. Nhat reached for it but the butterfly flew forward just out of reach.

Ignoring the fear that had previously overcome her, Nhat chased after the white butterfly. She felt a kind of warmth as she followed behind it, and even the soreness in her legs seemed to fade in the creature's wake. All she could think about was staying in the presence of this beautiful being.

72

The butterfly led her to the intersection, hanging for a moment as if making sure Nhat was following it before turning left and floating out of view. Nhat picked up her pace and turned the corner onto the busy street. People were starting their day and the streets were starting to fill up. Ignoring the sounds of the road—the various roars, honks, and squeaks of the cars and bikes passing by—Nhat scurried up the sidewalk chasing the white butterfly that seemed to glow brighter than the sun.

She huffed as she ran, holding the backpack straps tight so her cargo wouldn't bounce off the backs of her little legs. The butterfly danced around people in front of her, none of them caring to notice the magnificence of its brilliance. Nhat never took her eyes off it, dodging the same people it flew around and keeping pace so that it was never more than a meter in front of her. Nhat knew exactly why she was running after it. She wanted to catch it.

Nhat loved butterflies already, but this one was different. This one was magical. She knew that if she caught it, she would be okay. It would protect her. It would guide her. It would lead her to her family. She knew it when she saw it. This was the key to making everything better. This was how she was going to find her family. The butterfly would protect her from The Evil. The butterfly would make everything okay.

The butterfly stopped for just a moment. Nhat could have sworn it looked at her, but she was so out of breath and disoriented from running that she wasn't entirely sure. It flew off again, this time into the cross traffic of a busy street.

While she desperately wanted to catch the magnificent creature, Nhat approached the busy street with caution. Bikes, cars, and motorcycles flew through the intersection with no one directing them. The cross traffic took off whenever it saw an opportunity or whenever it made an opportunity of its own. She looked to her right and left and saw other people walking like her, waiting for the right moment to cross. Many were crossing with the traffic, forcing the cars and bikes to swerve around them as they made their way across the street without a care in the world, even for their own safety.

Nhat felt herself hesitate again. Looking to her memory, she recalled how she crossed streets like this before—always with her parents or her big brother. One time when she was five or six, the traffic was so chaotic that her father picked her up and ran with her instead of holding

73

her hand and showing her how to navigate such busy streets herself. It was rare for him to pass up an opportunity to teach something like that.

She could wait and rely on the traffic lights to assist in her crossing, but traffic rules were more of a strong suggestion here; if there was an opportunity to go, a car would take it. Nhat looked straight ahead and saw that the butterfly had continued down the sidewalk, towards the sun. She could still see it; even against the morning sky it glowed brightly, though its size diminished as it flew onward. She could still catch it, she thought, but her brain told her she had to move now.

Captivated by the butterfly, she looked quickly to her right and left and stepped out onto the street.

She felt herself yanked backward onto the sidewalk. "What do you think you're doing?" someone shouted. "You're going to get killed! Where are your parents?"

Nhat looked up to see a police officer holding onto her backpack. Though he wasn't exactly tall, she felt that he towered over her. His face was stern and his grip was firm, but it belied a gentle nature—that of a protective father, rather than a domineering authority.

"Where are your parents little em?" The officer's face relaxed and he released the backpack, understanding that she would not run.

Nhat had never been one to lie maliciously, but her brother had taught her to lie out of self-preservation. The lie came out naturally, like a fountain spring bursting through the rocks after centuries of erosion.

"They're over in that building," she said, pointing in the general direction the butterfly was heading. "I was being bad and they walked ahead without me to teach me a lesson."

The police officer accepted this without question. Unknown to Nhat, he had children of his own and understood well the sometimes-unorthodox methods parents used to teach a lesson to a chronically misbehaving child.

"Ahh, em, why so disrespectful to your parents that they would leave you to cross the street on your own?"

"I kept jumping off the sidewalk to make them scream," Nhat twisted her hands in anxiety as the butterfly floated further away, "but I promise not to do it anymore, Anh. Will you help me cross the street?"

The police officer smiled at her innocence, falling immediately for the lie. He took her by the hand, lifted his whistle, and blasted it at such a volume that Nhat almost covered her ears.

He stepped out with her onto the street, his whistle and authority as an officer demanding all traffic to slow down and allow them to cross. While cars and motorbikes whizzed past behind them, the pair were protected as they crossed. No one would dare hit an officer escorting a little girl across the street. Not even in a time of war.

As Nhat walked with the officer, she noticed that the butterfly hadn't flown as far as she thought. It would still be within reach if she ran as soon as she got to the other side of the street.

"Which building are your parents in?" the officer asked.

Nhat looked up at him. She had just pointed across the street before and hadn't thought this far ahead. She realized now that the police officer might want to escort her to her parents and have a talk with them. She started to panic.

"Em, which building? So I can take you there." They had reached the other side of the street, and he stopped to look at her. He let go of her hand and put his hands on his hips, waiting for an answer. Nhat didn't have an answer, the only thing she could do was what her brother taught her and keep the lie going out of self-preservation. She started to cry.

"Why do you cry little one?"

"If my parents see you with me, they will punish me for bringing shame to our family." She let the waterworks flow and pointed to the building nearest to the butterfly. "They're over there, but if they see I troubled a policeman they will punish me harder."

The kind officer nodded, hands still at his hips. "Yes, they will." He looked around, uncomfortable with what he was going to do but what knew was right. "OK, OK, wipe your tears away." He took a handkerchief from his back pocket and offered it to Nhat. "But go to your parents straight away, OK?" He patted her head gently. "Don't spend too much time out here by yourself. It's dangerous enough for a little girl all alone on the street during peacetime, and it's even more dangerous during a war. We don't know when the enemy is going to invade, but it's only a matter of time. Promise me that you are going to go straight to your parents and behave."

75

Nhat sniffled and wiped her face. "OK, Anh, I promise." She tried to return the handkerchief but the police officer waved it away, motioning for her to keep it. "Thank you for helping me cross the street," she said, bowing slightly.

"It's ok, em," he straightened up, "go on, before you cause more stress for your parents."

Nhat nodded and hurried down the street. She didn't run, but her pace was brisk and focused. She made it to the building she pointed out and noticed that the butterfly was halfway down the block, fluttering in the same spot she had last seen it. She reached the door and tugged at the handle; it wasn't locked. She turned to look back and saw the officer waiting for her to go inside. Nhat waved and he waved back. She knew he wouldn't go until she went in, so she took a deep breath, opened the door and stepped through.

Chapter Eight

It was dark inside. Daylight had begun to creep in, but it hadn't quite filled the space with enough light to see. Nhat took a deep breath and stayed as silent as she could. She didn't know where she was or who else was in here, so she stayed as quiet as a mouse.

She looked around and saw that there was furniture in the building, but she couldn't make out if it was for a home or an office. Standing still by the door she had just silently closed, she hoped no one had been roused and that she could count to one hundred and leave. By then the police officer would be gone and she could be on her way. Butterfly or no, she had to keep moving. She cursed herself for being so transfixed by it that she had forgotten why she was out here in the first place. She had to escape the city. The soldiers were coming and so was The Evil. She had to keep moving.

The butterfly had flown towards the sun. She was mesmerized at how beautiful and bright it was, even against the coming of day. Nhat thought again about the creature but quickly focused her mind instead on heading east. She thought about how much further she needed to travel before night came. Her thoughts turned to The Evil and when it would come again. The Fox had told her that it would not relent; she needed to find a place to stay the night and hide from it.

Looking around, she thought that an empty place like this would suit her well. *How do I know if it's empty though?* she thought.

The thought floated out into the air and hung there as if waiting for a response from some hidden inhabitant. The hidden soul who was roused by the door opening or the one who had just woken up, stepped out for some air or a cigarette and then came back in to start their day. The person who would come and find Nhat and turn her over to the police, or worse: keep her there and do all the things that her mother warned her someone would do if she ever wandered out alone, torturing her until The Evil showed up and ate both of them alive.

77

In her veins, the blood stopped flowing. Nhat was once again paralyzed momentarily by a fear of the world that she had in her mind. The fear that her mother had implanted there through repetition and the fear of the unknown monster that hunted her down.

Eyes shut against these thoughts, Nhat forced herself to count to one hundred. After one hundred she would peek her head out the door and if the officer was gone, she was going to make a break for it. Somewhere open, somewhere safe, where she could take a sip of water and look at the map to figure out where she was and where she needed to go.

She took a silent deep breath, looked down and started to count.

One. Two. Three. Four.

Bit by bit she began to relax. The breathing along with the steady rhythmic counting helped stabilize her body, which was wrought with anxiety fueled by excitement.

Eleven. Twelve. Thirteen. Fourteen.

The terrible thoughts slowly faded from her mind, and she felt her arms relax. Slipping gently from the straps of her backpack until they finally hung by her side. Head and neck soon followed suit and gravity pulled her head lower as she continued to count.

Forty-one. Forty-two. Forty-three. Forty-four.

Nhat's tiny legs also benefited from this exercise. She felt them become lighter and less tense as she continued to count, taking deep breaths there in the silence. It felt to her as if she were resetting her body and all her worries and aches were melting away. She continued to count slowly and breathe deeply.

Eighty. Eighty-one.

Her mind completely at peace now, save for the numbers, she felt her body follow suit and grow calm. Her body was here with her now, ready for whatever came after she was done counting.

Ninety-eight. Ninety-nine. One hundred.

Slowly, Nhat opened her eyes and found herself staring at the white tile on which she stood. It was slightly brighter in the room, the sun creeping in as it continued to rise.

She allowed herself a moment to wiggle every part of her body, take one last deep breath, raise her head gently and once again look around.

Nothing. No one. Not one thing out of place that signaled anyone was there. She nodded, gratefully, took a small breath, adjusted her backpack and slowly opened the door to peer out and see if the police officer was still there, waiting for her to betray herself.

***

Nhat had already been very lucky on her journey thus far, though she had no way of knowing it. The family whose home she had just wandered into were upstairs, still soundly sleeping. The concerned police officer had indeed been watching that door after her, only just turning the corner seconds before she'd stepped back outside. The enemy army was in fact preparing its advance on the city as she was leaving it. One lucky break that she *was* aware of as she left the building was that the angelic white butterfly was still there, flying around a post, waiting for her. Nhat knew this was the case because as soon as she stepped out it circled around her three times and flew down the street, again towards the east and the rising sun.

The light sparkled in her eyes. It was as if a star had come down from the night sky and did not realize it was daylight. It hung around and stayed by her, her own personal shooting star.

This time she didn't run after it. The butterfly stayed just ahead of her and Nhat kept a brisk pace behind it, watching it while also staying more aware of her own surroundings, careful not to run into the street and draw attention to herself again. There were many things she did not know about being out and about on her own like this, but she was learning quickly. She felt her mind growing sharper and learned to look at things differently than she had when she was just a child walking with her parents. Even her brother, just a few years older than she was, offered a certain level of protection. Here, alone, she had to be quick in mind and body.

The butterfly led Nhat straight eastward for a few hours. When she slowed down, it seemed to notice and guided her to a park just a few minutes down the street. There the butterfly landed gently on a light pole nearby while Nhat down and ate the second and final bao.

Hanging almost directly above her, the sun baked the city and its inhabitants. It was always hot this time of year with summer approaching.

Nhat was sweating as she sat underneath a tree and ate. She sipped on her water generously, but not so much that she would run out or have

79

to find a bathroom in a rush later—something that could put her in danger if she wasn't careful.

There was nothing to see here, really. The thrill of being out and about on her own had waned. All she had seen for the last few hours while heading east was the hustle and bustle of a city that was painfully aware that war was coming and there was nothing they could do about it. She saw soldiers everywhere, paying her no mind as they looked off into the distance, smoking their cigarettes and talking nervously. Black rifles that the Americans had given them hung off their bodies, waiting to be used against an enemy who didn't need American money or weapons to win. Nhat knew the enemy was winning because that's why her parents were always fighting. The side that they wanted to win wasn't going to, and that's why her mom wanted to go. To escape. To go somewhere that they could be safe.

Now she was going by herself. She thought of that as she slowly chewed on the second half of the bao. She would be escaping to safety and her family wouldn't be with her. Days ago, this would have brought her to tears. Right now, in the sun, in this park she didn't recognize, she could only think of the facts and not feel any of their accompanying fears that plagued her since her family had disappeared.

"Or left you," she mumbled to herself. She let the thought simmer and continued to eat the bao in silence until it was gone. A bird chirped and she looked up, gazing around at the beauty that was the day. It stunned her that the day could be so beautiful and dark as well.

Careful to ration the water she had left, Nhat took a sip and relished how the cool liquid washed the food out of her mouth and wet her parched throat. "I need to find water," she whispered as she capped the bottle, placing it back in her backpack. "I need to find somewhere to hide and sleep tonight too."

When she'd heard her own voice earlier while talking with the police officer, she realized that she hadn't spoken to another person in some time—only to The Fox. She realized that she missed talking to other people. She had spent the day muttering things to herself just to hear her own voice. Worried at the possibility of appearing crazy, she started looking around before she thought out loud now. After the police officer encounter, she didn't want to draw any more attention to herself.

Of course, a little girl walking by herself in a city preparing for a siege naturally drew *some* attention. However, for that same reason, no one paid her more than a few seconds' mind. Everyone was hustling to get ready for the coming invasion, doing their best to secure the things that they needed to protect those that they loved. If not that, they were in a rush to leave themselves. Either way, the little girl walking alone with a backpack that was way too big for her was the least of their worries.

There in the park she had caught a few curious glances, but people were far too weary to give her too much thought. Nhat watched the people who glanced at her. Many were traveling with bags, cars were loaded with possessions, and those on bikes carried large backpacks on their person. It appeared to Nhat that they were doing the same thing she was. They were leaving.

"Maybe I should follow the crowd," Nhat said as a pair passed nearby on a motorbike. The girl turned to look at Nhat, as if she'd heard her. Her black hair was flapping in the wind, and she had a look of sadness in her eyes as she sped away. Maybe it was for Nhat or maybe it was for herself. Nhat wouldn't know as the bike was soon out of view and she would never have a chance to ask.

"I should go," she said to no one, but her legs objected and wanted her to remain seated for just a little while longer. The day's long walk and the previous night's terror were taking their toll on her.

There was a feeling radiating through her body that she hadn't felt before. It wasn't exactly a physical pain, but if she could localize it the sensation would reside in her chest. It was a kind of discomfort that stretched out into every fiber of her being, including her brain. She wanted to scream out, but she also wanted to recoil underneath this tree, curl into a little ball and cry her heart out. In addition to all of that, she simply wanted to lay there and stare off into the distance and do nothing. She couldn't explain how she was feeling all of this at once, but there it was.

"How come?" she whispered to herself. "How come?" she asked again, this time to her feet and the dry dirt she sat on. "How come." This time it came out as a statement. Flat. Sad. Defeated in the wind. The words hung in the air as if spoken to exist in that space in front of her. It added weight to the air. Charged it with electricity. Yet all Nhat could do was sit and feel this feeling she had in her chest.

81

Scared, sorry for herself, angry, hopeless and bewildered, she put her arms around her legs, drew them up close and buried her face in her knees. There were no tears but rather a shallow breathing dictating everything in her being, telling her to stay and feel this pain for just a little while.

If time were to pass the same way she was feeling it, hours would have gone by and the sun would be on its descent, ending its reign over the day as a merciful God that had decided to temporarily cease its punishment of those who lived by its providence. However, as with everything natural in this world, time operated on its own schedule and did not yield its functionality to the whims of one human's suffering. Especially considering she was just one within one city, within in a country, within a region where everyone was suffering as she was.

Nhat finally looked up, disappointed to see the sun in the same place it had occupied when she put her head down.

The murmur of the city was the same, too. Everyone was moving about, doing everything they could to either prepare for the coming invasion or escape it. As the day went on she saw more and more soldiers, and fewer and fewer people like her. People who were just living their lives, hoping to be alive when this was all said and done.

"Alive." She let the word leave her lips. She knew the word. She knew what it meant. She also tried to ignore the fact that if she didn't move, it would no longer apply to her. That The Evil would find her and rip her limb from limb alone in the dark. And if it wasn't that, it would be a soldier who would knowingly or unknowingly hurt her, just another person who didn't make it. "They didn't make it," her mother would say when reading letters or the newspaper. Simply shaking her head and clicking her tongue as if the ones who didn't make it had brought in mud on their shoes when coming into the house.

"I have to make it," Nhat said, placing her face into her knees once more before forcing herself to stand up. Her legs stretched and ached as she slowly rose to her feet. Her back muscles tightened and then relaxed as she stretched her arms forward, her forearms and fingers feeling the last of the aches and the last of the relief.

Standing there blinking, Nhat took stock of what was around her. The world spun onward and so did the people in the city. No one was paying attention to her. For that she was both heartbroken and grateful.

She looked up at the light post to see if the butterfly would notice that she was moving and guide her to where she needed to go.

It was gone.

She looked from side to side. To other posts that held lights. To poles that held bundled jumbles of electric wire. To the trees all around her. She even looked down at her feet to see if it came near her and settled down to have lunch with her.

Everywhere she looked was ordinary, and the extraordinariness of the brilliantly beautiful white butterfly was gone. For a time it had brought her out to parts of the city that she had never seen before, nor dared to visit without her family. It was her special guide, and now it was gone. It had guided her well, though: Nhat knew in which direction she was heading, and for now that was enough. Once she got to the edge of the city, she could look at the map and follow a route to the coast. For now, she would just keep walking.

She sighed, picked up her bag and continued to the east.

***

The sun eventually went from heating the top of her head to warming up her back. The afternoon brought no relief from the heat, but it at least helped to not have her little head, covered in black hair, feeling as if it were on fire. The backpack took the brunt of the sun's warmth and only the back of her little arms and little legs were aflame. *That* she could handle better than her head.

Half the water was gone. She hoped that she could find a jug somewhere that she could sneak some from or find a faucet where she could replenish her supply. If that was the case, she could fill up her bottle and drink straight from the faucet that night and the next morning, making her water bottle last a little longer.

Nhat walked straight ahead for three more hours. The city grew less and less dense, but she knew she was still far away from the coast. It would probably take her another day to simply get out of the city, maybe two in total to get to the coast. Hopefully she could make it. Hopefully the soldiers wouldn't attack. Hopefully she could hide from The Evil.

"Hopefully I can find my family," she said, with a hint of anger behind that simple sentiment. The anger wasn't directed at them, but it was

83

growing to the point that they would be included in its blind wrath all the same. It spread slowly inside her like a growing pool of acid that must one day be poured out or overflow within her.

As Nhat walked the anger began to slowly creep away. It had risen in a way that she recognized the feeling, but for now the love she had for her family had done away with the feeling. After all, she still hoped to find them.

The glances she stole at the people she passed were both out of fear of them and hoping to catch a glimpse of the people she so desperately wanted to see again. She wondered repeatedly if it would ever happen. The thought would leave her mind, allowing her to focus on the road in front of her, but her grief would bubble up eventually and force the thought back into her conscious mind randomly and frequently. She was caught in a box, one in which every time she bounced off the walls she thought of them.

She started to speak again, but only sighed. As the air left her lungs, thoughts of The Evil came to mind once again. The sun was getting lower. That meant that night was coming and with it The Evil that was out to kill her in one of the innumerable grotesque ways her imagination had conjured for her, willingly or not.

A chill ran down her spine, exacerbated by the day's sweat. The beads of perspiration turned to ice as they trickled down her body. In the depths of her mind, she heard The Evil growl, and she pounded the concrete harder, walking briskly as if it were following her in the shadows beginning to grow on the streets.

There was no way to tell either way if it was near her or not. All she could do was let the fear that had chased her out of the house and into the unknown guide her.

She remembered The Fox. Just like the white butterfly during the day, it too led her in the dark of night. She wondered where it was now, with its white shiny coat and –

"Wait," Nhat said out loud and stopped. "It was white too." Her head tilted up and she recalled her memory of the previous night and this morning. "They both shined bright."

Nhat saw The Fox and The Butterfly together in her mind, both shining with the same light. In the darkness, The Fox was a source of light and safety. In the light of day, The Butterfly was a source of beauty and wonder.

The two must have been related. They shone the same light and although they came at different times of day, they came to do the same thing, guide her. Guide her from –

Nhat gasped. The feeling she had just earlier from believing The Evil was in the shadows returned to her. If The Fox and The Butterfly were guiding her, it was because evil was not far behind.

Twisting around with a flourish, Nhat turned to face the sun behind her as it sank closer and closer to the horizon. Night was still four hours away, but the shadows of the taller offices had already begun to stretch and consume the smaller buildings around them, casting the alleys between them in an ominous twilight.

Her little dark brown eyes strained to see anything that resembled the beast from the night before, made from maggot flesh and baring the smile of a human being as its massive yellow eyes bored directly into her soul.

While she trusted her eyes, she turned to her other senses to detect what couldn't be seen. Nhat closed her eyes and took a deep breath, hoping to calm her nerves but instead hearing The Evil's unmistakable growl.

She stood steadfast, ears open, hoping to gain any information that could be useful to her. It growled again, its guttled noise seeping through the streets as it stalked her in the afternoon shadows.

"It's still far away," Nhat whispered to herself. Another growl was the creature's reply; low, curdled and wet, and devoid of any human empathy.

Nhat opened her eyes, looked to the sun and placed her hand in front of it. She knew she had some time left to find shelter, but she also knew that the shadows would continue to grow until then, giving The Evil more space to explore and hunt.

Nhat looked around for The Butterfly and The Fox but knew they would come in their own time and that no matter what, she would still have to move quickly in order to take advantage of the remaining daylight and find a place to hide.

She didn't know where she would go or what she would do. All she knew to do right now was move and put as much distance between her and the thing growling for her in the shadows.

Without hesitation and with fear as her guide, Nhat turned once again to the east and ran.

Chapter Nine

Night was around the corner, and so was The Evil. As Nhat ran, the creature took long, slow, deliberate steps. Bugs and rats crawled out from underneath their hiding places as The Evil stalked the city, sniffing out its prey as she made her way across streets and avenues. In the afternoon shadows it found its opportunity to renew its search, taking care to avoid the light that burned the wriggling mass which served as its flesh.

It snaked around buildings, crawled over and underneath cars, slinked around patches of warm sunlight, and flattened itself against walls by changing its shape. If one were to observe it moving and how it navigated against something as omnipresent as daylight, they might mistake it for something like an octopus that had somehow found its way ashore.

As it was, however, no one could see the creature except for those being hunted by it. Those who it yearned to consume.

Nhat had seen it last night. She felt its presence this afternoon. The only thing she could do was try to escape it. She didn't need to be told that it wanted to devour her—she understood that ever since it first appeared in her father's office, banging on the doors, watching her as she looked for the dictionary, waiting to tear her limb from limb.

She didn't know what to do now except run and keep an eye on the sun as it continued its inevitable descent towards the horizon. Stopping from time to time, she would walk around the nearest block and try to see if there was a place that she could stay for the night.

Finding nothing but locked doors and boarded-up windows on the ground level, she would take off running again, looking and hoping for something to appear as the afternoon light began to grow gentle and the sweat on her brow began to feel tepid and cool.

The edge of the sun—the one that bit with the promise of daylight and safety—was diminishing, and so was her time. As the shadows lengthened and grew so too did The Evil's range of motion. When Nhat would slow down to walk sometimes, she heard its growl in the distance, that guttural rumble that sent chills down her spine and flight into her legs.

Night hadn't yet fallen, but desperation began to fill her little heart once again. It crept into the rest of her body, her legs willing her to give up, sit on a corner, and wait for whatever grisly fate arrived to claim her. Her mind, at least, was still full of resolve, and it was her mind that dictated to her body what to do.

One foot in front of the other she scurried, desperately trying to find a place to hole up for the night. She didn't need comfort, she didn't want the appearance of safe, she wanted only to be inside when it was dark and to make as little noise as possible. To wait for The Fox and live another night to trek to the coast.

Her back felt cooler, she looked back to the west and saw that the sun was now nearing the horizon. It would be completely down in two hours, maybe less. She didn't know. She only knew that night was coming and she was out of time.

"Walk faster tomorrow, right now run," she said out loud as she turned east and made another break for wherever it was she was destined to be.

The spurts were half sprints, and half power walking strides. To anyone watching it was a random and spastic display of confusion, the antics of a child who had been out in the sun all day. To Nhat, it was an act of desperation and fatigue. She didn't want to go on. She wanted to lay in her bed at home and eat sweets until she got sick and then scolded by her mother while she held her so that she would feel better. Instead, she was out on the streets trying to outrun a demon. Demon. *Why use that word?* she thought to herself.

"That's what it is," she responded out loud.

She stopped, sweat dripping from her forehead, this last mad dash taking more out of her than she realized. There in the middle of the sidewalk, on this side of town that was devoid of traffic, she plopped down her backpack and took out her water bottle.

The gigantic gulp she took soothed her throat and immediately cooled down her small body. Some of the water ran down the side of her face, cooling her cheeks and neck as it drizzled down. Though it was warm, it felt as if ice water had met her skin. She raised the bottle straight up and brought it down with a dramatic flourish and gasp. For a moment, she felt better.

After a quick look around to make sure no one was nearby, she carefully took out a pack of dried meat and fruit. She removed one piece of dried pork and a handful of dried mango and pineapple. The fruit she threw in her mouth all at once and the piece of meat went into her left pocket for easier access later. Nhat carefully arranged her backpack's contents again and placed the water bottle inside. As she let the fruit moisten in her mouth, she rehoisted her backpack, and slowly turned to face the west to watch the rapidly setting sun.

The orange glow filled her with a mixture of happiness and melancholy that she would forever feel at this time of day. It was the color she would see with her father whenever they went on nature outings, of the sky when her mother was bringing in the laundry from outside, of the backdrop against which she and her brother would play on summer nights. The memories would remain, and so would the pain.

"Pain." She mumbled the word around a mouthful of food. Her mother wasn't here to scold her. Her dad was not here to slap her mouth. Her brother's rueful jokes were nowhere to be heard.

She felt a hatred boiling inside of her, something that told her to blame her family for what was happening and to never forgive them. This feeling burrowed into her heart, taking root so she could hate them forever. Even if they did ever find her again, she would hate them.

She chewed the now moist fruit. The acidic bits of pineapple overpowered the peaches and bits of mango that were meant to give the quick meal a broad tropical palette. Her tongue tingled.

"I should go back," she said out loud, bits of fruit flying out of her mouth as she stared at the setting sun. "I should go back and let it kill me so they can feel bad." Her little fists tightened around her backpack straps, her jaw clamping down angrier and angrier with each bite. "They should know that they left me and that I died because of them." She was about to launch into how she wanted to see them cry when she suddenly felt a stabbing pain in her mouth. She yelped out in surprise and let a stream of half-chewed fruit and saliva fly out.

The mush hit the sidewalk with a wet thud. Nhat clutched at her cheek, the source of the new pain. She stood in silence for a while, rubbing her cheek with her hand while poking around inside her mouth with her tongue, looking for a wound. Her cheek was hot on the surface, a mix of the pain and the sun beating on it all day. Inside her mouth she felt a small hole in the bump that was quickly welling up.

Pain had left her mouth as a word just moments earlier, and now pain resided within it. Nhat was incredulous. She knew that her foul words and thoughts had caused this, and she was sorry for it. She was sorry to her parents and brother. She shouldn't have said those things. She felt tears welling in her eyes, but the sadness disappeared just as quickly as it came.

Nhat stood staring at the ground as twilight came rapidly approached behind the fading afternoon.

To a passerby she would just be a girl staring at the ground. A more curious person would see her staring at something on the ground before her. Someone who was brave enough to approach and ask if the girl needed help would see her staring at a pile of fruit mush. But only Nhat could see what it was she was staring so intently at. Not the sidewalk, or the mush: it was the small pool of blood from her cheek that she'd spit out with it.

Nhat felt the air grow cold as the light began to fade around her. Shadows stretched and consumed the street, and she felt her heart beating through her chest. The blood on the ground, the same blood that rushed now into her heart and throughout her tiny body, had a smell, one that The Evil that hunted her in the distance would pick up on.

The growl was unmistakable. Her fear became more pronounced. Nhat had not yet found a hiding place, and now the creature that chased her had picked up her scent. Because of her hate, because of her anger, because of the sadness that fueled these other emotions, evil in its purest form now had a tail on her.

She did not run. She simply turned and walked down the street, heading east. She heard the growl in the distance, felt the change in the air. The Evil was coming from her, and Nhat was perfectly aware.

***

She had three options, as far as she could see.

The school with the sizeable hole in its fence. She was small enough to easily squeeze through. Getting into the school itself, she wasn't sure, but maybe she would luck out and find an unlocked window or door somewhere. She wouldn't know until she tried, but she'd have to commit to it before that.

The second option: a restaurant that had long since been closed down. Nhat knew that she could get in through the back; she'd circled the building several times and saw that there was a broken basement window. There would probably be standing water and snakes down there, but that was something she could deal with. She would at least have a chance against snakes.

The third option was to keep running and hope that The Fox would find her soon. While that was an option if she had nothing else to work with, it had already been an hour since she bit her cheek and she knew that her blood on the ground had narrowed The Evil's search for her considerably. She zig-zagged and sprinted when she could, but her exhaustion caught up to her and she eventually came back to the same conclusion: if it found her blood it would eventually find her.

She thought it best to listen to The Fox, find a hiding spot, and wait for it to come. She knew it would, she just didn't know when.

Nhat took one last look at the setting sun, only its top still glowing above the horizon. In thirty minutes it would be gone completely, and she would be alone in the dark. She had to make a choice on which way to run: the restaurant or the school.

The restaurant was a small building crammed in among many others, with lots of shadowy spots where she could easily move from building to building if needed. The school, however, offered a larger area in which to hide and longer distances to run in case she was found out. While this wasn't her school, it shouldn't be laid out too differently from any other school, so she could probably navigate it better than a bunch of buildings that she didn't know.

The sun twinkled as it continued to descend. The orange cream sky had turned a light pink, a color she enjoyed but could not stay to appreciate. Nhat sighed, watching the sun's safety slip away. She took a hurried step forward and made her way to the school.

***

The sound of thunder was even more surprising than usual since Nhat had not seen a single cloud in the sky all day. She had always been terrified

91

of thunder, and the sudden claps caused her to fall from the top of the fence she was climbing and land hard on her hands and knees, scraping them badly. Her pants ripped and she felt hot liquid accumulating.

"Blood" she said out loud.

Her heart raced as she looked to the sky to see where the storm was. She dusted herself off, picked up the backpack that she'd thrown from the top of the fence, and wiped the sweat from her forehead. Even in the early evening, the heat combined with physical activity caused her to sweat profusely. The clear skies indicated that there was no rain coming, and there was no drop in temperature or delicate scent of flowers that thunderstorms always brought with them.

The night was still stale. She didn't smell flowers. She didn't feel cool. No, this was –

BAM. BAM. BAM.

Explosions rattled in the distance. In the short time since she had heard the thunder, she didn't have time to think about what else the sound might be. In fact, even after the subsequent explosions, she referred to the initial sound as thunder.

Terrified by the sound in the distance, Nhat looked to the horizon where she heard the thunder coming from. She looked for clouds and rain, anything that would explain what she was hearing. Maybe The Thunder Bird her dad had told her about had come back to claim the world like it was foretold. She squinted and gazed around frantically, scanning for clouds and a giant bird who would reclaim the Earth as its own.

But she didn't see a storm or the hundred-meter wingspan of a giant mythological bird. Instead, she saw a series of flashes which were followed by the loud thunderclaps that came in succession one behind the other.

CLAP. CLAP. CLAP. CLAP. CLAP. CLAP. CLAP. CLAP. CLAP. CLAP.

Ten times. Ten times the thunder clapped one behind the other. She was thinking what that could mean when she heard ten explosions in the city, one behind the other.

BAM. BAM. BAM. BAM. BAM. BAM. BAM. BAM. BAM. BAM.

Nhat normally wouldn't be able to see the city in the dark because everyone turned their lights off on account of the war, but there in the early evening, the fires caused by the explosions slowly lit up buildings she

92

had seen earlier that day. The orange light gave them a mesmerizing glow as they appeared to dance in the light. Windows came into view as black holes, doors as gaping portals to other worlds. The light shone into the buildings and the outside glazed like a beautiful mango that was just right. The flames danced and so did the smoke that rose from the piles.

That is when she realized the horror of the situation. She didn't hear it at first, but it soon rose out of the city with the smoke that was filling the air. Screams.

The screams of people who were running from their homes. The screams of soldiers running to prepare for battle. The screams of bad men who were coming from where the thunder originated, ready to bring what everyone had feared and finish what had been going on for Nhat's entire lifetime.

The war had arrived in the night. Nhat stood as the fires burned, as people screamed, and as a demon inched its way towards her in the darkness, ready to take her life.

Chapter Ten

Nhat ran into the school. It would be the last foolish thing she would do. She knew she had to get away from The Evil, but right now she had to get away from The War. There was no time to think. In the time that it took her to run to the school and find a window in, The War had already thundered more than fifty times, with more than fifty explosions following. The screams of the people in the city rose into the air like a poison gas cloud that threatened to suffocate anyone caught in it.

She heard machines and men from both sides of the city screaming, running towards each other to do whatever it was that men did in war. The War was here now. Though she had heard so much about it, her innocent mind couldn't comprehend what The War was. All she really knew was that it was dangerous and that if she didn't escape it, she would surely be killed.

The War was here, and The Evil was on its way. Which would kill her first? She wondered as she stood in the dark and empty school.

She tried four windows before she found an open one, and even then she could barely open it up to scurry through as each clap of thunder brought more screams and each explosion made her flinch in succession.

She scraped her knees again on the sill, spilling more blood from the already bad scrapes. She did her best to clean the red liquid off the sill but with each thunderclap and explosion she flinched and flinched and finally shut the window to shut out the horror that was the night.

The War went on outside, but inside it was mercifully muffled. Inside the thunder didn't hurt her ears. Inside she couldn't feel the fear from the people's screams. Inside, she was safe. For now.

Instinctively, she squatted down and took off the backpack. She placed it in front of her, took out the water bottle and took a good long gulp. She only had less than half left; she would fill up here in one of the restrooms or the school kitchen.

She wiped her hand on her sleeve. In doing so she realized the odor she was giving off.

"Maybe I can shower here," she thought out loud, scanning her surroundings. She was in one of the classrooms. There was nothing that indicated that students studied there. It had long been abandoned.

She couldn't remember when she'd last gone to school. They closed them down when they started talking about The War coming to the city.

Nhat put the water bottle back and took out her flashlight. All the lights inside were off, and she didn't want to risk turning one on. The flashes outside illuminated the classroom just a little bit, but it wouldn't be enough to see. She could turn the flashlight on and off again and avoid drawing attention to herself. There were men with guns and bombs that looked like thunder at first and also a demon out to get her. If she drew attention to herself, one of those things would get to her and she didn't know which would be worse: to be blown apart or to be ripped to pieces.

She stood up, feeling the fresh pain in her knees. The blood was beginning to stick to the fabric. She knew she would have to change soon and if she couldn't shower, at the very least clean her wounds.

Backpack closed and flashlight in her hand, she moved to where she'd last seen a door, saving the precious light for the darkness that waited in the school's halls.

***

The fresh scrapes and cuts rubbed raw against her ripped pants. The warmness had gone and had been replaced by a cold feeling that agitated her flesh.

The school's windows offered a little bit of moonlight along with the flashes from The War outside. As she walked, she followed the pale light that was reflected dully on the dusty floor. Nhat looked behind her and saw her footprints in the dust. It had been a long time, then, since anyone had been in school, she thought.

She clutched the flashlight tight against her chest and quickened her pace. She was used to what a school was, but she wasn't used to the dread of being alone in one in the dead of night. With a war raging outside and something hunting her as she bled at the knees. There was fear in the air and if you asked her, she wouldn't be able to tell you if it was hers or if it was the atmosphere of the empty school. It seeped into her lungs,

95

causing her heart to beat faster. The fear fused with the oxygen in her lungs and dispersed into her bloodstream. That blood flowed to her legs which walked faster, to her arms which lowered and swung in a power walker's fashion, to her brain where it dominated her thoughts and told her to "run."

With a flash of thunder, an explosion from outside, and the sudden shattering of the glass in the hall, Nhat burst into a full sprint and ran for her life.

She switched on the flashlight and held it like a knife with the blade pointed away from her. Nhat reached a single door and threw it open, coming to a larger hall that only went right. She hit the wall, turned and shone the light on The Evil that had finally found her. She saw its yellow eyes flash and the sickening glint of its human teeth. It recoiled at the light's touch, throwing its head back and standing on its hind legs, howling a bloodcurdling scream. It shrieked like a bird, with the glottal accent of a lion and the clarity of a man screaming in pain. She didn't hesitate any longer and ran down the hall at full speed, aiming to reach the end and throw herself out of whatever door or window she could find that would lead outside. As she got closer, she could make out a single door at the far end.

Legs pounding the tiled floor beneath her, she glanced around to see if The Fox or The Butterfly were nearby, ready to save her again or show her the way. There was no sign of them, or the white orb of light they had originated from. Nhat stole a glance behind her and saw The Evil standing at the end of the hall on all fours, rearing its head and gnashing at the air.

She pumped her legs harder, knowing that soon it would be on her. To stand still was to die. To move was to live a moment longer.

The door was a few meters away now. She could make it, but she knew that if she stopped to open the door the monster would grab her. There was no time to question it—she picked up her speed the best she could and leapt at the door.

She closed her eyes and waited to land on the other side. Instead, her little frame smashed against the door and she crumpled to the floor like a rag doll. Pain radiated through her whole body and her face went numb. Before she could think she was lifted into the air, her legs and arms dangling below her. The Evil had picked her up by her backpack and she dangled helplessly as she saw the floor shrink beneath her.

This was it. The Evil had won.

"Take your arms out of the straps and fall!" a voice shouted.

The Evil screamed and before Nhat could see who had given her the command, she did what she was told and fell to the floor. She landed with a thud, her face smacking against the tile. She felt blood rushing from her nose, but she didn't reach for it, scrambling to her feet and running for the door. She threw it open and found herself in the main lobby of the school. Her little head whipped around, droplets of blood flying, hair sticking to her sweaty face. She gripped the flashlight for dear life and searched frantically for a way out.

A loud roar came from the hall behind her, rising over the thunder and the continued explosions from outside. She scanned the area and ran for the front door, but it was locked tight. She ran for a window and found it, too, immovable. The Evil's stomps echoed from down the hall. She saw the front reception desk and jumped over it, opening the door behind it that led to the headmaster's office. She closed the door softly, ran over to his large desk, crawled underneath it and clicked off her flashlight.

There she took deep, slow breaths, attempting to calm her heartbeat and reduce the amount of noise she was making while gasping for breath. Her whole body trembled but with each heavy step she heard outside the door and with each breath she drew, she felt herself gain control of her body and, thus, her fear.

The air grew cold and stale. It reminded her of when she was at home, looking for the dictionary in her father's office. She took one final deep breath and exhaled slowly, the same way she would when she was listening to her parents fighting or was bored at the monastery. So much air escaped her lungs for such a tiny being, but not a single sound went with it. Her body became still and relaxed, and although she could feel her heart thumping to escape her chest, the whole of her being became numb.

As the final puff of air left her lips, she saw it crystalize in the air. She smiled slightly as her breath became a puff of smoke that floated off into the darkness.

Her skin began to crawl. The brief smile faded, and she brought her knees to her face and hugged them tight. She could smell the iron in her blood. She inhaled slightly, taking in the aroma of one of her favorite

97

smells. The "salty" taste and smell that she always referred to whenever she had a small cut on her finger and licked it before her mother could stop her.

Mother would always chastise her for that, telling her it was disgusting, but those were the moments where Nhat didn't particularly care what her mother thought. She enjoyed the taste of her blood whenever she got small nicks here and there.

It likes the taste of your blood too, a voice said in her mind, bringing her focus back to the bitter cold seeping into the room and the fact that The Evil was just on the other side of the door.

The stomps outside were not those of a rampaging beast or animal; the being moved with a purpose. Each thud on the floor was a step that fell just a bit closer to her. It inched its way outside of the office carefully, methodically, each step a signal that it was looking, waiting, thirsting, for her.

Silence fell over the school. The thunder outside and the lightning flashes from the explosions had stopped. The artificial storm created by The War had taken a momentary break, the screams subsiding. Here in their microscopic part of the universe, the world was quiet.

The Evil snorted—it had stopped moving. Nhat closed her eyes and gripped the flashlight, ready to blast light on the creature and make a run for it if need be. The War was just as scary, but she would rather deal with that than take on The Evil without help from The Fox and the ball of light that it was so afraid of. She wondered where they could be but decided to focus instead on making a plan, should it come bursting through the door.

She pictured it standing there in the main lobby sniffing for her, its body slithering in the moonlight as the worms and maggots that made up its flesh writhed all over. Its yellow eyes piercing the darkness, scanning for traces of her. Its lipless mouth, grinning with murderous desire and sickeningly perfect human teeth. Its claws clutching her backpack, with all that she had left in the world.

Nhat patted her pocket and felt the main set of documents inside. She could still try to flee the country, but she probably would not make it very far without the supplies in the backpack. The keepsakes from her family were in there as well, captured by a monster that didn't know or care for their significance, its composite flesh crawling all over the last bits

98

of her family that she had left. The thought of trying to get it back briefly came to mind but left it just as quickly. She was lucky to escape with her life. She had her papers. That was enough.

She buried her little head into her knees and wrapped her arms tighter around her legs. Completely still in body and breath, and bewildered only in spirt, she waited for what was on the other side of that door.

Home came to mind. She thought of sitting in her little fort with the flashlight where she waited for The Evil to come out of her father's office, before she knew what it was and that it was after her. She tried to think of the warmth of the place where she used to feel safe, but all she could remember was waking up one random morning all alone.

Now she knew why her father didn't want to run away. Running away was hell.

Nhat yearned to go home, but now that she was being stalked by The Evil and The War had finally come, that was terribly unlikely. Her focus right now had to be on staying hidden and staying alive.

The air was growing colder by the minute. Nhat wanted to shiver. Her teeth wanted to chatter. There was very little she could do to stave off the cold but wrap around herself tighter.

The cold meant that The Evil was getting closer. There was no way out of here. The light would help, but only so much. She would have to break out a window, or sprint back the way she came and hope for a miracle, or –

The door cracked open. The air became as ice. The hairs on her neck stood up. Nhat's eyes opened. There was nothing she could do. She heard The Evil step in, and it stood silently at the door.

Two more tentative steps were taken into the room. She heard the labored breathing that was surely excitement coming from its lungs. In the dark and silent room, she could hear the wetness of its moving flesh, its wicked tongue licking its teeth, its breathing that came out in husks of wheezes and gutted gasps, and the floor creaking under its weight.

Nhat gripped her flashlight and held her finger over the button. She relaxed her body and let blood flow through her limbs. There was only one thing she could do after she jumped back from beneath the desk and shone the light on the demon's face.

She was going to have to run.

99

Part Two – The War

Within

Responsibility meant getting to your post without getting screamed at. Showing your superiors that you were capable of not being an utter failure, that somehow you deserved to be here in this hell with them. Responsibility, to you, was neat, simple, and quick, if you could just shut your mouth and do it. Be here, be there, but most importantly, be on time. That was responsibility.

Shine your boots, clean your weapon, maintain light and noise discipline. That was responsibility. Everything else fell into place if you were responsible. Everything was nice and neat if you were responsible.

Then the war started, and suddenly being responsible was some made-up bullshit that the higher ups used to break you so that when you were told to get down, you got down. When you were told to open fire, you opened fire. When they handed you a pistol and told you to execute the unarmed prisoner, you walked over and shot that kneeling man in the back of the head and smoked a cigarette after, thinking nothing of it other than "Man, this is a clean shooting pistol."

You spit. Not on the truck, but on the street. Because you're responsible.

These were the words thrumming though Sergeant Do Duy[1]'s mind as his unit sped down the road in a column of other trucks. An artillery barrage was going to come sometime after night fall. It was already late afternoon, and most of the units had already been placed around the perimeter of the city in order to engage the enemy. This unit was a last-minute addition. They were to attack the artillery units themselves in order to ensure the least amount of damage to the city. They knew there was little time, but they had no idea that the enemy's barrage would commence as soon as the sun went down. The North had finally come to their beautiful city. They all knew that it would take a miracle to push them back, but all the same they were going to try.

---

[1] In Vietnamese culture it's customary to put the surname first.

Do had spent eight years of his life fighting this war, he wasn't about to just let it go now that they had been pushed all the way back home.

All the same, when he saw the flashes in the distance he couldn't help but feel a sense of dread, as if this was his last night on Earth. The explosions came a short time after. The small delay while the shells took time to find their targets created a silence so eerie that not even the trucks in which they sat seemed to make any noise.

They all watched in horror as the city they loved so dearly and were tasked to protect exploded in the distance. Silence was all they could offer.

"Get ready," the radio crackled through the hot night air. "They're already advancing in some areas. We might not get to the battery."

The radio cut off and the trucks all rattled as the soldiers within made sure they were ready for a fight that would come at any second.

Do took one last drag of his cigarette, flicked it away, and began to give instructions to his men. For he was, in fact, a responsible soldier.

Chapter Eleven

Do scraped gravel off his face. The truck had nearly crashed into the wall of a school they decided to station at when an artillery shell struck the column, forcing the drivers to turn every which way. He jumped out as the vehicle struck, causing him to hit the ground.

One of the shells took out the second vehicle. The other five took that loss as an opportunity to get out of the way and scramble. It was one thing to be a target of an artillery strike, it was another to be the target of an artillery strike when they had you zeroed.

Do got up and dusted himself off. His M16 rifle, left behind by the Americans, had fallen a few meters away. He went to retrieve it and turned to survey the destruction that the artillery shell had caused on the truck carrying some twenty men. There were bodies and parts of bodies everywhere. Many of them were unrecognizable. They would have to go and collect the body parts to see who they could identify. To see who was still whole. There was no time for that now, though. Right now he had to get everyone who was still alive ready for a fight.

"Spread it out! Don't get zeroed!" Do shouted into the cacophony of voices and artillery bursts. There were explosions near and around him, but they were so far spread out he knew the enemy had no sights on them. Yet.

He walked back to the truck and helped his men out as they took stock of the area around him. "Nguyen," he said, "The radio." The soldier who carried the heavy pack passed him the receiver as he hopped off the back of the transportation vehicle.

"Two-One Actual, this is Two-Two, we were targeted by artillery. Interrogative, what are our orders." He listened for a moment as the men from all the trucks filed out and spread themselves out over the school grounds. Many of them were checking to see if they had been hit, others were preparing themselves by surveying the area. They were going to be in for a fight.

103

"Copy that. Two-Two out." Do handed the radio back to Nguyen and turned to his men. "Ok, listen up! Artillery is not our target anymore. We're to secure this area and prepare for advancing infantry. Private Hua."

A younger man came running forward. He was carrying a machine gun, the kind that mowed people down like grass.

"Take a fire team and secure the roof of the school. Set up positions facing south of us here. Send back a runner with a report."

"Yes Sergeant," the young man said and ran to secure a team.

"Secure the school and set up a perimeter," Do slung his weapon over his soldier and took out a cigarette. "We wait for those bastards here." He took a long drag, looked around the place and finally went to go inspect the pile of dead bodies that littered the school parking lot.

No one had said anything, but in that wreckage was their Lieutenant. A man who, after all he had seen, was still afraid of dying. A liability in a war that everyone now knew was ending starting today.

Do went up to the burnt remains of the truck and looked in. There he was, in the passenger seat. His skin was charred black and his mouth was stuck open as if he were screaming. Where his eyes had been were two black holes peering out. The driver was the same way.

He felt bad for the driver and the rest of the men who didn't make it. He felt bad the Lieutenant had died, but it was a feeling tinged with relief; the cowardice of that man would have led them all to an earlier grave. They way were all headed toward an early grave regardless, but if he could postpone that just a little bit, then he had done his job as both a responsible adult and soldier.

He stared a little longer at the driver and the Lieutenant. He didn't want to, but it was something he had to do. He stood up on the door frame, reached in and pulled out the dog tag that was still hanging on the driver's neck. It was charred, but it would be able to be cleaned and confirm his death. He stepped down, walked over to the passenger side, and did the same with the Lieutenant. The dog tags would bring comfort to their families in knowing that they had died and weren't rotting away in a prison cell or unmarked grave. Death wasn't welcome, but it was sometimes preferable.

He slapped the frame of the cab and walked away. Since the Lieutenant was dead that meant he was in charge now. He knew this war was ending soon, but that didn't mean he could just abandon his men, his

104

post, or his duties as the lead NCO. There were things to be done and that included honoring the dead. He saw two men trying not to look at the wreckage; they would have to do.

"You two." He threw them the dog tags. "Dog tags. Pick them up." He didn't look them directly in the eye nor wait for them to protest. He gave the order, walked on and made mental notes on what needed to happen for them to launch a successful attack.

The first thing was to secure the school. The second thing was to —

BAM. BAM. BAM.

The gunfire was from one of the rifles that a regular rifleman would carry, like his.

RATATATAT.

That was from the machine gun Hua carried.

"On me!" Do screamed as he raised his rifle and ran towards the main doors of the school. He didn't look back to see if his men were following; he knew they were, even if he couldn't hear the rapid clatter of their boots on the stones outside.

It couldn't be more than a patrol of NVA, the main forces hadn't reached them yet. Maybe they could get some useful information and —

A roar rang out over the courtyard of the school. The shooting had stopped and there was silence. Do stopped dead in his tracks and so did his men.

They saw the silhouette of a man lurch toward the door. He stopped, pushed it open and fell forward.

Do was about to run towards him when he saw it.

The figure stood at least three meters tall. It looked as if someone had skinned a gigantic bear, its flesh glistening in the moonlight. The entire surface pulsated, almost as if it was moving, its sinewy texture reflecting light from the bright moon.

Do had never cursed a clear night before, but standing there looking at this monstrosity, he wished for complete darkness. Even if he couldn't see the threat, at least his memory would be spared the sight of such a creature.

The men stared, each of them witnessing the pure, absolute horror that stood before them. Two yellow orbs appeared in the darkness. It was

105

staring down at Private Hua, lying motionless on the floor. Whether he was already dead or just near it, Do didn't know.

As he thought about calling out, the creature raised its head, shone its yellow eyes at Do and his men, and smiled.

Living through eight years of war had numbed Do to the horrors that humanity had to offer. When he saw the creature smile, he felt afraid for the first time in a long while. It bore human teeth, perfectly straight and grinning at them through its lipless mouth. Do looked at the creature in earnest. Its flesh was in fact moving, comprised of what looked like maggots and earth crawlers. Its legs and arms were powerful, each limb ending with prominent claws. It stood on its hind legs, smiling at them, grinning as if feeding off of their fear.

"THE GIRL! Save the girl!" Hua had pushed himself up and screamed his final words at them. At this moment the creature lifted him by his head, screaming. They watched in morbid astonishment as the creature lifted him up and brought him close to its face. Before the monster could finish what it had started, Private Hua pulled the pin from a grenade and shoved it into the creature's mouth.

It bit Private Hua's arm off with a snap. Blood sprayed everywhere and Hua screamed as if he had all the lives of everyone who had died in this world in him. He screamed for everyone. He screamed for himself. He screamed until he no longer could. The creature crushed his head in one swift movement, dropped his body and turned to smile at those in front of him. It took a step forward and its chest exploded. Its eyes went dim, it fell to its knees, and slumped to the ground.

Silence.

The grenade had gone off. Private Hua killed the creature in his last breath. Whatever it was, it was –

"It's getting up. Sergeant Do, it's getting up."

All four of its limbs propped it up as it looked down and slowly rose. They watched as its chest closed up once again. The creature looked up at the group; this time it wasn't smiling. Its yellow eyes bore into them with an otherworldly hatred. It flexed its arms and legs, gnashed its teeth, and snarled as its flesh pulled itself back together.

"Sergeant Do, what do we do?" one of his men asked. Do couldn't answer, still transfixed on what was before him.

"Sergeant, what do we do?"

The creature had fully healed, its anger and thirst for their blood apparent. It brought its front limbs down and stood on all fours. Its back was arched, claws dug into the ground, and its teeth were borne for all to see. It was going to attack.

"Open fire!" He didn't hear himself saying the words, but he felt himself saying it as he lifted his M16 and began to shoot at the demon in front of him.

His men didn't hesitate. The volley of automatic bullets hit the creature square in the chest. Bits of its moving flesh tore off it and even one of its eyes was hit, shutting it as the creature recoiled from the barrage of fire.

Do himself reloaded a magazine during all of this, the rate of fire continuing at it let him know his men did the same. No one stopped firing until the creature dropped to its knees and fell.

With a grand thud, the grinning demon fell again to the ground. There was silence in the square, with only the distant machine gun fire and screams from the inner city to remind them that they were in a warzone. For Sergeant Do Duy and his men, it felt as if they had stepped off their trucks and into another world. They didn't know what was in front of them, only that they had killed it.

Do wasn't going to take any chances. He checked his weapon and replaced a magazine, retraining his sights on the creature. His men followed suit.

"Two columns. Three fire times fanned out up front, three fanned out in the rear. I want column one to take positions around it ready to open fire, second column will go up to the body and unload a magazine each on it. Fire teams stand by to support." He threw two fingers forward and his men organized and headed toward the immobile creature.

To watch this unit of men move was to watch a dance, carefully orchestrated through discipline and respect for each other. Respect borne out of a sense of brotherhood that only physical conflict could bring during such dark and ruinous times. Most of these men had known each other for a few years, some had only just got on towards the end. No matter the timeline, they had all learned to love and respect each other for the sake of the work at hand: winning the war.

That objective was about as far from their minds as it could be right now. In absolute shock and fear, they marched silently and quickly

107

towards something so heinously unbelievable that their brains wouldn't let them fully comprehend it until they were sure it was dead. Human nature dictated after all that in order for something to be understood, it must not be a threat.

The first fire teams arrived and took their positions by the school doors and surrounding area. Their weapons trained on the creature, they watched as the first column surrounded the beast in a large semicircle and the second took positions just in front of it in a tight circle. The second set of fire teams positioned themselves behind the group, mirroring the positions of the first set of teams. Sergeant Do Duy himself joined the circle of the second column and trained his weapons on the creature.

There was a silence that cut through the ranks, a silence these men had all heard before. The kind that tells you something just isn't quite right. The silence that always seemed to kill.

"Fire."

Heeding that silence, Do and his men fired into the creature at point blank range. The sound of their rifles was deafening. The bullets tore into what was now apparent as the flesh of the beast. They were a mix of maggots, worms, centipedes, snakes, and anything else that this world commanded to crawl on its belly. They were the same color, each varying a slight degree. Bits of them flew off as the bullets shredded the carcass. There was no blood, but instead a putrid and pale-yellow liquid oozed from the wounds. The smell was as revolting as its appearance.

The barrage only lasted a few seconds. Before anyone could speak or reload, Do gave the command. Second column reposition, first column joins me. The men moved in synchrony. The second column reloading along with Sergeant Do and the first taking their spot around him.

"Fire."

The second barrage produced more flying bits of torn flesh and yellow liquid oozing around them. After the second volley, Do ordered the two columns back and told the fire teams to each unload one magazine into it. He stood two meters away and watched as each set of three teams took their position and shot the creature into oblivion.

Satisfied, he sent the men to secure the area, to make sure that no patrols had been sent to investigate the commotion. He was sure that the NVA wouldn't attack once he met them to show what they had found. He was confident that this would end the war right here and now, that the two sides would come together in order to find out what this was and flush out any others that were lying in wait for them.

Sergeant Do would begin to wonder. He took a seat on one of the truck's beds and sat to stare at what was on the ground in front of him. He lit up a cigarette and let his imagination get the best of him. For the first time in a long time, he let his mind wander. It was a dangerous thing to do in a war. It meant that you were sloppy, it meant that you would miss a detail that would come back to bite you, it meant that you could die.

Death is surely what would have occurred if Sergeant Do's mind continued to wander. In fact, he almost did something that would have cost someone their life if he didn't have years of training and focus.

Lost in his imagination and wandering thoughts, he didn't see what came out of the school's front door. At least not right away.

Had it been a replacement sitting in that truck, or someone who was feeling jumpy, a tragedy would have occurred—a tragedy they had seen many times throughout this conflict. One that his own comrades had committed over the years of warfare, that caused a break in their minds so severe that they would never come back from those depths.

When he finally registered the movement, Do instinctively raised his riffle and pointed it at the target. He stopped however, when he finally *saw* what had come out of those doors and walked past the creature that lay dead on the ground.

A little girl, bloodied in the face, looked up at him with big black eyes that welled with tears.

"Is it really dead?"

Chapter Twelve

People who knew Do as a soldier would have never agreed, but a third-party observer might say that Sergeant Do almost shot this poor child.

All at once Do had remembered everything before shooting the creature to death. He remembered Hua coming out, screaming his death knell that rallied the men to kill whatever it was that so callously devoured him. Do remembered how Hua yelled, "The girl! Save the girl!" right before that creature bit into him and ripped him apart.

The eight-year veteran had to push that image out of his head as it came to the forefront to distract him. He'd had to do this before. He had forgotten his first kill, the woman he strangled who he met in battle, the tank running over the top part of his best friend at the time who was trying to get away with a bullet wound in his leg, the civilian village that had been napalmed by the Americans, and now this singular image of horror he would never be able to describe.

Do looked down at this pretty little girl who was battered, bloody, and from the look in her eyes, dead tired.

"Is it gone, anh?" She looked up at him with eyes full of fear and resignation, but also the sparkle of just a glimmer of hope. "Is it really gone? Did you kill it?"

He nodded, shocked. It was clear this girl was being hunted by the creature from her looks and the fear in her eyes. He didn't know what to say.

Kneeling down, Do took a pack rag out of his side pack and wet it with water from his canteen. He reached for the little girl to wipe the blood from her face, but she took a step back in fear.

"It's ok em," he showed her his unit patch on his sleeve, "We're the good guys."

"Good guys?" she asked timidly.

"That's right. We're here to protect you from the bad men who are coming and…" he stole a glance at the creature laying on the ground. Once

110

again, he was drawn in by what he saw there on the ground, what he had seen do just moments before.

"And what?" asked the little girl.

"And whatever else we need to protect you from, little one." He extended a hand and held up the rag. "Come, let me clean your face."

The little girl wrung her hands and looked around, half timid and half fearful. She stepped forward.

Do remembered his little sister back home, her coyness that always seemed to show up when strangers came around. He smiled, pushed away the memory, and began to wipe the girl's face gently. He was looking for other wounds but was pretty sure that this blood had come from her nose.

"Where is your family, em?" Do asked instinctively as he wiped her cheeks on either side.

The girl didn't answer. She stood still, held fixed in the same position so Do could clean up her face. He looked at her eyes, hoping to see a trace of something hopeful, but saw nothing. He had seen that face in kids before, kids walking up to him asking for help, crying, sometimes naked, sometimes missing a limb or an eye, sometimes dragging a dead sibling. He could tell you with near certainty where this girl's family was. He didn't press it.

"Where else are you bleeding from?" He had learned to ask kids simpler versions of the questions he really wanted to ask. *Are you wounded, did you come into contact with anything toxic, is there shrapnel that needs to be removed, do you need medical attention?* The things kids would know the answers to if only they understood the questions.

"My knees," she said, lifting her chin so Do could clean the rest of the blood that had run down her face. Do smiled at the quick answer he got. *Easy when you know how* he told himself as he poured more water on the rag.

"Do your legs hurt when you walk?"

"Nope." she replied softly.

"Does it feel like a stick pokes you when you breathe?"

"Nope." She took a deep breath for him as a demonstration.

He chuckled, "Do you throw up anything black or red?"

The girl didn't reply, she simply shook her head back and forth in a dramatic motion, letting her hair fly and whip him in the face.

111

He let himself laugh and so did she. The two giggled as he finished wiping her face. Smiling at her laughter and playful nature, he was satisfied that there were not major wounds on her face. He would get to her knees in a minute.

"What's your name, em?" He always saved this question for last, once he got them laughing or smiling. After all, who gives their names so willingly in a world that's trying to take it from you?

"Nhat. Nhat Ngoc Thien." The girl said softly. She smiled, frowned, looked down and around and added, "I don't know where my family is." She began to cry softly, wringing her hands again while looking down.

Do wiped away her tears and spoke softly to her. "There, it's OK, Nhat. We'll find them." He took out his canteen and offered it to her to sip. Nhat took the canteen and softly drank from it, being careful not to spill any of the precious fluid. "When was the last time you saw them?"

"Four or five days ago," she said, sniffing and handing back the canteen to him.

Damn he thought to himself. "I'm sure we can find them," he lied. Wanting to take her mind off of that, he asked "Does your stomach make angry noises?"

She laughed and shook her head, "But I am hungry," she said. Her voice dipping the way kids do when they need to elicit sympathy.

Do smiled, thinking of his little sister yet again and pushing her from his memory. He stood up and slung his rifle, extending his hand to hers, "Come on," he said, "let's go get you something to eat."

She took his hand and followed him to one of the trucks.

***

The men had gathered around shortly after Nhat started telling her story to Do. In a few minutes, Sergeant Do and his men learned where the creature had come from and that it was indeed hunting this poor girl who trekked the city trying to escape it after her family had disappeared. They learned about the orb of light, The Fox, The Butterfly, and that what she called The Evil had grown half a size larger after it ate their comrades.

One of the men went in the school to see if it was true that they were devoured. He returned with only their rifles and a backpack that the

112

girl exclaimed excitement over when she saw it. Apparently, all that she had left now was in that bag.

No one questioned her story, for the body of the beast lay on the stones just outside of the school's entrance. They had seen it rip their friend apart and devour half of him and had killed it themselves. The existence of the orb of light, The Fox, and The Butterfly were more or less readily accepted as well, as she had made it this far on her own. After all the evil they had seen in this war, it was nice to believe there was some shred of supernatural good in the world.

The men had sympathy for her. Sergeant Do, on the other hand, had respect. He didn't know many kids who could do what she had done on her own and survive this far, but here she was, alive to tell the tale. He shuddered to think what would have happened to her if they hadn't show up, as it was about to come into the office where she was hiding. *Would she have been able to escape?* he thought.

He looked at the child, Nhat, for a long while, regarding her while she ate. She sat cross legged on the stones outside the school, a fireteam surrounding her while the rest of the men secured the perimeter. He smiled; the girl had her own guard of men to protect her and she didn't even know it.

Sergeant Do was hesitant to leave her. He looked around the area and assessed the situation from where he stood. The school itself was secured, but none dared approach the entrance where the beast lay on the ground. The fire from the truck had long since been put out. The artillery strikes in their immediate vicinity had ceased for now, and the sound of gunfire reached them from different parts of the city. There was resistance on all sides. It would take the night before the reds could come in and take the perimeter. By morning they would have the city. By then he would be dead.

Will she, though?

Do looked up at his men standing around her. "You three, go inside and secure a room for her. Someplace likely not to get hit, someplace anyone can get to her if we fall back."

"Yes, Sergeant," one of the men replied.

The three took off and it was just Do and Nhat again. The child munched on a piece of barbecued pork they had made earlier that day, alternating bites of that with a rice cake she held in her other hand. It was her second serving. He regarded her for a long time before finally speaking.

"Em, where are you going?" The topic had not come up yet. Many assumed that she was just running, but Do was worried about where she was running to. Not because he was being nosey or curious, but because if his hunch was right, where she was running to was as about as dangerous as the demon that lay on the ground just a few meters away.

Nhat chewed on the piece of meat thoughtfully. She swallowed and looked at up at him. Her big dark eyes zeroed in on his. He knew what she was doing, because he was doing the exact same thing. They were seeing if they could trust each other. She chewed on the piece of meat, took a bite of the rice cake, thought some more, and swallowed before she finally replied.

"I'm going to be with my family," she stated.

"Yes. But how will you get to them?" Before he could continue, he heard something that sent chills down his spine.

"Someone help me! Please! Don't let me die like this!"

He turned and scanned the area, but there was no one. He was sure of what he'd heard. He looked at Nhat, who was looking around as well, wide-eyed with a mouth full of food. The other men in the area had heard it too.

The voice was Private Hua's, who had been killed by the beast.

"Please! Anyone! Don't let me die here!"

"Hua! Where are you?" someone shouted from the roof.

"I'm inside! I'm inside!"

"Where inside?" Sergeant Do yelled out, picking up the rifle that he had leaned up against the wheel of the truck.

"Inside!" Private Hua shouted out for the last time before his voice changed into something else. A low rumbling began to shake the ground beneath their feet.

"Inside of you," a growling answer came as the earth began to tremble beneath them. "I am inside all of you, and you will all be a part of me."

The rumbling intensified as men began to pour out of the school. Mixed shouts of "Get ready!" and "Here they come!" were heard, along with "What the hell was that voice?" and "It's starting to move!"

Sergeant Do Duy and Nhat Ngoc Thien were both frozen in place. Do stood with his rifle raised at the creature while Nhat sat with a mouthful of BBQ pork and rice cake, neither saying a word.

Do looked down at Nhat and Nhat looked up at Do. They both turned to look at The Evil. Slowly, methodically, it began to move, the flesh that had been shot off crawling towards it. Its limbs began to twitch first, the bits of flesh finding their way to the appendages and attaching themselves again. The Evil began to lift itself up, its low grumbling thickening into a growl, to the horror of everyone watching who had just had a hand in killing it. Or so they thought.

Fear gripped Do's heart. He looked around and saw that half his men were watching what was happening and the other were watching something else. Something that he should have been focused on this entire time but, between the demon and the girl escaping it, had failed to remember it was on its way.

The War.

He watched in a stupor as one of his men up on the side of the road, who had been trying to get his attention, fell as a bullet entered his chest and exited out of his back. He turned to see The Evil on all fours, his men firing again at it.

The gunfire came from all directions. A mix of M16s and AKs firing at different targets. Half his men firing at The Evil, the other half at the NVA, and the NVA firing at him.

No more than a second or two had passed before Do snapped to, grabbed Nhat's arm and pulled her up off the ground.

"Run!" he screamed at her as he pushed her forward. "Take cover in the school. I'll find you!" he nodded and began to open fire into the enemy that had found them.

He cursed at himself, between the "killing" of The Evil and them listening to Nhat's story, he allowed them to remain utterly exposed. The enemy had a vague idea of where they were, the rain of bullets they laid down confirmed it, and their lack of focus doomed them.

There would be no coming out of this, between The Evil and The War, they were stuck. He didn't have enough men to repel an attack and he certainly didn't have enough men to put that demon down permanently. They were going to die, all there was to do was to decide how.

115

"Fall back! Everyone fall back to the school!" he shouted, as he backed up and reloaded his weapon. The NVA had five trucks of men unloaded and firing upon them. He had a plan, he just needed to get everyone inside. "Fall back into the school damnit! Now!" He turned and ran.

The Evil was still on all fours, its body healing and reorganizing itself as his men continued to shoot at it.

"What are you doing?! Fall back into the school!" he shouted at the men shooting at The Evil. "Leave it for the reds!"

The men, understanding now what he was doing, nodded and ran into the school. The others who were engaged with the NVA covered each other but lost men as they fell back.

Do returned fire from the corner of the building, covering his men as they fell back to the school building. "Find the girl!" he shouted as they ran past him, "Regroup in the auditorium!"

By now most of his men were in the building; some five or six didn't make it. He saw their bodies on the streets. There would be no going back for their dog tags. The War had arrived and so had The Evil. This was their end; he was sorry to leave them that way.

In the dark he could see a wave of men approaching. He turned and ran to the building. Taking a good look at The Evil, he saw that most of the flesh that had been blasted off had reattached itself to the body. He stopped to look at it, kicked it over and looked into its eyes.

They were wide open and burning yellow. The lipless grin was tight and angry, it was very much alive and very much furious. Do could see fire in its bright yellow eyes, burning for revenge.

"My people are coming to kill you," he said and spit in its face. "Men who look just like me." He spat at it again and ran inside.

"Close the doors and barricade them with the desk," he ordered. "Find the girl and get everyone into the auditorium," he added and turned to see The Evil turn on its side, forcing itself to get up. The doors closed and the last thing he saw was the mass of flesh standing up, flexing its arms, curling its claws, gnashing its teeth in the air, and a mass of NVA soldiers in the distance followed by a tank.

116

Chapter Thirteen

The first tank shell burst just in front of the school building. Between the roar of The Evil and the screaming outside, Do knew that the enemy had encountered the monster and were focused on killing it just as they did. He didn't know what was going on exactly, he didn't want to know, all he knew was that he had just bought them all a few moments before either The Evil came after them or The War did.

There would be no guarantee of who would be left standing to kill them. Maybe a well-placed tank shell would truly take care of The Evil and the swarm of red that was about to rush over their poor country would do it, or maybe The Evil would prevail, slaughter all of them, and continue its hunt for the girl.

"You," he pointed to a man who was standing wide eyed with fear, "make a run through campus, get everyone who's not here to the auditorium." He looked at the man next to him, who had the same look of terror in his eyes. "Go with him, but you keep an eye out for the girl, make sure she comes with you." The men nodded and ran.

"Everyone to the auditorium," Sergeant Do unslung his rifle and strode to the place where they would regroup, rearm, and reconsider their strategy. The War was here, and it was clear for some time now that they couldn't win it. He didn't know what had awoken inside of him, but he was now hellbent on getting his men out alive and the little girl to safety.

"Sergeant," one of his junior men ran up next to him, "what do we do about that thing outside?"

"Let the reds handle it," he said, turning to see the large portion of his men that remained but noticing just how many were now missing. "How many men scattered, how many casualties?" he asked. The junior man next to him shook his head, he turned his head to the right for an answer but received none.

They all strode on in silence.

***

It wasn't often that Do breathed a sigh of relief, but when he saw the majority of the men standing there, some of the tension eased off. Sitting on a table, flanked by six of his men, was Nhat. Do nodded, as if telling the unforeseen forces that allowed for this reunion and reorganization that he agreed to whatever it was that permitted them to take a moment and think about what was going to happen next.

The men gathered around him as he entered. The auditorium had been cleared of its chairs and the stage consisted of nothing but the card table that Nhat was sitting on. It wasn't so much an auditorium as it was an all-purpose room, but nevertheless that's what most of these schools called them.

No one dared to speak. Speaking meant that they had an idea of what was going on and wanted clarification; right now, no one knew what was going on and they waited for direction from their commanding officer. If they only knew he didn't have it for them.

"We have about five minutes before Hell meets us at this gate," he told them as he checked his watch. "One way or the other we are going to fight something here, and I don't know if it's going to be those bastards and their tank or that thing after it's ripped into all of them."

No one spoke. Do continued.

"So, the reds we stand a chance against, but we might have to fall back. The beast, as we know, grows after it has eaten." He looked at the girl, "You're sure that it was a little bit smaller before, em?"

Nhat nodded eagerly and intently, glad to be a part of the conversation. She was holding the hands of one of his men, this made him smile internally.

"So that means if we end up fighting that thing, it'll be much larger than before because it will have gone through a lot of NVA. Which, for once, is not a good thing for us. If it's that much bigger, we'll have no choice but to fall back."

He looked around at all of them. Everyone understood what needed to happen, but no one wanted to suggest that they all retreat without putting up a fight. It was the cowardly thing to do, the dishonorable thing. However, with the war clearly at its end, their country lost, and one of hell's demons stalking them, what more could they do except save their own lives?

118

"OK." He looked around. "Anyone have a problem with doing that now?" He scanned the eyes of his men, none of them were looking down or away, they all met him back with a resolution that told him more than words could. It was time to go home.

"Squad leaders make a quick note, I want to know who didn't make it. Fire team leaders, organize your teams, that's how we're going to move. If we move as a big group we'll be a big target for artillery. We move as ants, we" –

A blast rocked the building. Everyone looked to where the sound came from and waited to hear what they were going to have to face. At first, they heard men shouting and the rumble of the tank advancing. A moment later there was a loud explosion, and a roar that made their blood run cold.

Do ran to Nhat, lifted her up off the table and shouted to his men, "Dismissed! Run!"

The flurry of activity was organized, chaotic, heated, and calm, as each soldier compartmentalized their fear and anxiety to let their training take over. As Sergeant Do Duy carried Nhat Ngoc Thien, he carried himself with a calm and focused demeanor. If anyone could feel or see what was going on inside of him, he thought, it would be the girl, Nhat. He had his arm underneath her bottom, her legs and arms gripped tightly around him, and her face wandering around the scene that was before them all. He wondered if she could feel the blood racing through his veins, the wild beating of his heart, and the fear he had at The War that raged outside and The Evil that stalked them between the flashes of artillery and passing of bullets. He wondered if he could keep this girl alive. He wondered if he could keep himself alive. He wondered for the first time, if he would see anything remotely happy ever again.

"When we get out," he said as he marched towards the side door of the room where his men were filing out, "we're going to have to run." He looked into her eyes and she stared back, finally nodding when she realized that he wished for her to answer. "I'm not going to leave you behind, but I can't carry you either. You're going to have to keep up and you're going to have to do what I say, when I say it. That's how things work when you want to stay alive. Less time thinking, more time doing. Understand?" The girl nodded and he turned to survey the room as he walked. His men split into two forces, one heading out of the auditorium

119

through the school entrance, the other through the side door, where he was heading with Nhat.

He didn't know where he was going to take this girl, he just knew that he had to get her out of here. They would have to survive a firefight if they found it, they would have to put that creature—or demon, whatever it was—down again if it followed them, but it was clear: they were going to have to figh. He personally would have to keep her safe. She was now his responsibility.

They filed out into the night, the sounds of gunfire and the creature reaching them from the other side of the school. Do considered his options as his men emptied out of the room. He could go deeper into the city and surrender with the rest of the general forces, making sure Nhat made it to safety. Or he could try for the coast. If the girl's family had disappeared, then she could make it out of the country with the countless other orphans and find a life somewhere else in the world. Sure, it would be difficult for her, but she had made it this far.

He heard boots clatter on the ground as he watched his men leave the school. Even though he had the girl, he wanted to be the last one out. It was his duty. He regarded the sound they made, as they filed out. It then dawned on him that he could hear them, that the sounds outside had gone out. He stopped to listen, looking to the other side of the school, Nhat turning in the same direction. There was no time to think, he put his hands around Nhat's head and dove for the ground.

This explosion leveled the building. Nhat screamed, her terror muffled by the ground and Do on top of her shielding her body from the debris that landed all around them. His men screamed as they ran out the remains of the school, shouting obscenities and firing their rifles at whatever target they were fighting. Do heard the tank moving, maneuvering to engage either them or the creature. Even above all the other noise and the ringing in his ears from the blast, he heard its roar. The Evil battled the NVA as the NVA fought off both the creature and his men. Shots rang from both sides. The War continued, and so did the carnage from hell. He would have to contend with both The War and The Evil. The War would chase them into the city, but not the coast; he knew the NVA was only interested in the capital. The Evil would chase them to the city as well, but would it be able to follow them once they got onto a

120

ship? He wouldn't know until he got there. What he knew now was that he and Nhat had to run.

"Em, em," he pulled her up. "Come on, we have to run!" Standing up, he grabbed Nhat's hand and ran to the wide-open door. Most of his men had made it out, but a few were killed in the blast. Some had pieces of shrapnel in their backs, their blood pooling on the floor. Nhat made an uneasy noise and hesitated. He picked her up and ran over the bodies, there was no time. "Don't look at them," he said as he ran over them and out into the dark, "close your eyes."

Outside it was a scene he was used to. War.

Fires cast distant scenes in an orange glow. Men hid behind wreckage and other bits of landscape that offered them shelter. Some fought, while others fled looking to save their own lives. It was a painting he had seen in the museum of his mind all too often. The canvas was hung up, viewed with horror, taken down and repainted, and hung up with a fresh new take on the same scene to torment him in ways he didn't think were imaginable. The artist knew what troubled him, what made him buckle at the knees. War had grown routine for the young Sergeant. The artist knew it was time for something new.

Another explosion rattled Do, Nhat and the rest of the men. The NVA stopped firing at them and focused their attention on the cause of the explosion. Do set Nhat down and edged along the side of the remains of the building. He instructed her with his hands and eyes to stay put and hugged the wall as he neared the corner. He eased his head around, careful not to make sudden movements that would draw the attention of the enemy. Bullets whizzed by in the near distance and men shouted in hysterics, trying to fight what Do already knew to be terrorizing them. He finally got into a position where he could see what the artist of war had painted for him today.

Fiery wreckage where a tank used to be, surrounded by NVA soldiers firing into it. Men on the ground, most of them missing their limbs, some with half their body torn away like Private Hua. There in the fire stood The Evil on its two hind legs, towering at four meters. Do thought himself crazy but it appeared that the beast had grown as Nhat said it would. He dismissed the thought, understanding that the existence of the demon in and of itself was crazy and such thoughts were perfectly normal at this juncture.

121

The Evil rained terror down upon the NVA, swiping at them with its jagged claws, ripping into their flesh as they fell back. Do watched as it grabbed a soldier by the arm and swung him with such force that he was thrown, screaming, through the air, his arm still firmly in the monster's grasp. Most of the NVA stayed back; they had seen the power this demon possessed as well as what little effect their weapons had on it.

Another roar burst forth from The Evil, sending Sergeant Do scurrying behind the wall again, away from his vantage point at the building's corner. He looked at Nhat, who was covering her ears in terror. He knew the road leading out of the city would be choked with NVA. There would be a fight whichever way they went, but there was little time to think about which one to avoid. He had to decide before fate decided for him.

"Come on," he screamed at Nhat over the noise, "this way, follow me!" Sergeant Do unslung his rifle and motioned for her to follow him. He set off for the perimeter of the school, towards the fence. There they would be able to slip away from the firefight and start looking for somewhere to stay holed up for the night. He didn't want to go too far back into the heart of the city; their ultimate goal was still the coast, they could make better time from here on the city's outskirts once the road was safe. They just had to hide.

"Where are we going?" Nhat asked. Her voice was small and frail and he almost didn't hear it. He turned behind him and saw that she was on his tail, keeping pace. Again, he was impressed.

"Far away from here," he said, his blood pumping as fear began to course through his veins, "but we have to find a place to hide for the night. We have a long trip tomorrow."

"Long trip to where?" she asked again, now running next to him. He regarded her small frame and how easily she was able to keep pace with him. She was smarter and tougher than the small innocent girl she appeared to be. He decided then that he wouldn't sugar coat things with her.

"To the coast," he huffed. "I'm going to get you on a boat and – "

A flash of heat burst across his shoulder. His legs gave out underneath him and he hit the ground. He didn't have to look to know what happened; he had seen it countless times before and everyone told him how it felt. He had just been shot. His left shoulder felt as if it was burning from the inside out.

As soon as he hit the ground he was clambering back up, using his rifle as a support. "Come on!" he shouted, "We have to hide now!"

"Are you OK?" She tried to see what had happened, but all she could tell was that he had taken a stumble and kept going forward.

"I'm fine," he gasped, "but we have to move faster, come on!"

They picked up the pace and ran into the night, jumping over fences, hiding in alleys, moving among the shadows, trying doors and avoiding streetlights.

Eventually the girl led him to a small restaurant, relatively out of the way. She had to crawl underneath the boarded up fence and behind the building for a few moments before reappearing in the front to let him in.

The adrenaline was working its way out of his system, and he nearly passed out once he finally sat down. He focused all his energies and told the girl what to do: how much water to get, what alcohol would look like, where to find some clean rags, and what to look for in his pack.

It was a small moment of rest and respite. They would stay there for the night and he would think of a new strategy now that he had this bullet wound to contend with. In the meantime, they were away from the fighting, and from The Evil. For now, they could rest.

He looked at the ground and noticed the mess he'd made, blinking back tears and weariness. Some rest would do him good. It looked as though he'd lost quite a bit of blood.

123

Chapter Fourteen

"Right, you're going to stick this in the hole and make sure that it burns all the flesh all the way around, OK?" He held the glowing red knife in front of Nhat.

He saw that she was paralyzed by the thought of doing what he was asking of her, but there was no choice. To cauterize the wound would stop the bleeding and give him a chance at getting her to safety, even after losing so much blood, but he could not see it to do it himself. He was lucky that the bullet passed straight through without hitting anything major; he was unlucky in that she would have to cauterize two holes rather than one.

"You're going to have to do it twice Nhat, front and back, and I need you to do it right. Do you understand?" She nodded. "Good," he nudged the knife towards her, "take it."

He took off his jacket and leaned forward.

"Stick the tip of the blade in the fire for a little bit longer." The small fire he created in a bowl they found would burn out in a few minutes, but it was enough time to do the job. There was always the risk of being seen, but the windows had all been covered up with newspaper and the fire was small.

He watched her as she followed his directions. She stood there, carefully holding the combat knife. Though her hands—both clasped around the large handle—didn't tremble, he could see in the glow of the fire that her eyes did.

"Good. Remember, you have to stick it in and get all around the circle." She nodded solemnly. Her body, still and confident, didn't betray any feelings that what she was about to do was beyond anything she had ever done to another human being. Her eyes, however, cried for the life that she had before.

Do wanted to get the exit wound done first; it was bigger and more ragged, and she would probably have to do it two or three times if she lost her nerve. It was going to hurt. A lot.

Next to him was half a quart of whiskey Nhat had found behind a pile of flattened boxes when she searched the building earlier. Do took a swig and saved the rest to disinfect his wounds. The torn edges of his flesh screamed when Nhat poured the liquid on, but he did not. He hoped this would be enough to save him from an infection.

He took the bottle from Nhat and set it back down next to him, for after.

He took a deep breath and looked at Nhat, standing there with the blade glowing orange at its tip.

He nodded. "Do it."

The pain was unimaginable. He expected her to hesitate, but she instead thrust the glowing blade into the wound on his chest where it had exited. She made eye contact with him and he saw the terror in her eyes. Heat radiated through his chest and back. He clenched his fists and pounded them together over the opening of his crossed legs. He could not scream for fear of being found out.

The smell of burnt flesh reached his nostrils, a smell he knew all too well thanks to the Americans' bombs. Tears streamed from his eyes but he remained silent, only exhaling a grunt as the blade was finally drawn away.

The girl stepped back and squatted, looking at him, concern in her eyes. He closed his eyes, wiped the sweat that had formed at his brow and nodded his approval.

"Good girl. Now do it again." He pointed towards the back with his thumb. "Then you're done." He sighed and kept his eyes closed. Leaning forward, he prepared for the searing pain that would again visit his body. He hoped the pain plus the amount of blood he'd lost would not be enough to cause him to pass out.

A few moments passed and he realized that he wasn't in agonizing pain. He peeked an eye open to see if he had died after all but instead saw the girl standing over the fire with the knife, reheating it. He had forgotten to mention that. *Good girl*, he thought and closed his eyes again, waiting for what was hopefully the last of the worst.

When it did eventually come again he strained against it, as if offering his back to the gods for sacrifice, his neck to the enemy for release, his very essence of being to the highest bidder if they could just take him out of this fucking world. The pain radiated through his back and damn near to his kidneys.

The smell of searing meat returned so strong that he could taste it, and he had the misfortune of now knowing what his own burning flesh tasted like. He wished he could joke and say that he tasted good, but all he could do was bare his teeth, clench, and take sucking breaths that offered him nothing except the knowledge that he was still alive.

Do felt Nhat gently remove the knife and then heard her set it down on the ground before sitting down near him. He waited a few moments, listening for noises from outside in case the light had given them away. After a tense few minutes, he took a deep breath and thanked Nhat for her help before making a new plan. They needed to rest and eat what little they could scrounge up, because the next day would be just as dangerous. The city had been invaded and a demon (*Or whatever the hell it is*, Do thought) was hunting them down. He had to know more about the other things she mentioned and why she was being hunted—but for now, deep shallow breaths.

"Em," Do finally said, slowly opening his eyes but still leaning back on his arms for fear of moving too much. "Where is the light now?"

Nhat turned to look at him. Her eyes glistened, but she wasn't quite crying.

"I don't know," she shook her head. "It usually comes whenever I need it."

Do nodded and closed his eyes once again; asking that one question took more energy than he anticipated. Now that he was resting and the adrenaline gone, his body took stock of where it was at, and it was not in a good place. He would make it, he thought, but he needed badly to rest.

A few good hours here and he would be ok—he just needed to be sure they were safe first. If the ball of light that she had told him and his men about was real then there would be no need for him to stay awake and be on the lookout, and he would be able to sleep clear up until morning.

He thought of his men gathered around Nhat not long ago, listening to her story. He thought about the others, who had died along the way. Those who he never heard back from. Those who were still alive, out there fighting the war and the monster chasing them. Do's eyes slowly

126

opened. He thought of them, all scattered out there, fighting one enemy they all knew and one that they knew frighteningly little about. His tired eyes fell upon his crossed legs. His tiger striped fatigues were worn, his boots dirty with fresh blood, his own blood on the floor...

Do's eyes widened. The blood—surely he had left a trail after he was wounded. They had to leave. If that creature could track Nhat all day with just her scent, it would be on them in no time. Panic rose into his chest as the prickly feeling of adrenaline rushed through his veins again. As he was about to shove himself up to his feet and call out to Nhat, he heard her speak.

"Hello again."

A gentle white light emerged from the corner of the room. It gently swept away the darkness, as soft as spring emerging from the dry ground, giving life to everything around it as it seeped in. The light wasn't bright enough to make him squint or worry about being noticed outside, but everything it touched could be seen. Do gazed at the light with wonder. He looked over at Nhat, on her knees with her hands in her lap and her head tilted slightly to the left. When he first saw her walking out of the school she was a scared little thing, but now he was seeing the gentleness she carried within her. The uncaring world hadn't completely driven out her childish innocence, not yet at least. She was still, at her core, just a little girl.

"How are you?" she bowed as she asked, a gentle and curious smile on her face.

Do turned to see who she was talking to, but the pain shooting through his shoulder objected.

"I am well, little one," came the reply. The voice was neither masculine nor feminine, but it carried the weight of authority and the softness of love in its tone. "I am well. Forgive me for being late. The War detained me."

"You were fighting?" Nhat asked, her gaze fixed as if she were speaking to the light itself. Do found himself too weakened at the moment to question what was happening, even if he were still of a mind to do so. Like a good soldier, he accepted the reality of his immediate surroundings and listened intently.

"No, my little one," the voice hesitated momentarily, lacking the capacity to sigh on account of its heavenly quality. "My involvement in this war is different, more passive. To say that I am 'fighting' would imply that I am losing."

"Oh," said Nhat. Do sensed disappointment and confusion in her voice.

"Nhat," Do interjected, diverting their conversation. "Could you help me to the corner?"

Nhat turned toward him, a look of realization spreading across her face as if she had momentarily forgotten his presence. She stood up and approached him, and as he extended his hand, she struggled to assist him to his feet. Do's immediate concern was reaching the corner where he could prop himself up; he would soon focus on whatever or whoever it was that Nhat had been conversing with. For the moment, finding a place to sit and rest was his primary concern.

The Sergeant, newly turned 30, took the small girl's hand as he finally managed to stand and made his way to a corner. There, a window met a pillar that protruded from the wall. This vantage point allowed him to observe the street through a hole in the newspaper covering the window, while also keeping an eye on both the back and front doors. He settled in to rest and provide watch—a soldier's duty.

As she led him to his chosen spot, he felt the world spin around him. Sergeant Do had been tested before, but this was the first time he unprepared for the challenge. Being a soldier was simple. Being a soldier in the midst of war was tough. Battling demons and trying to safeguard a little girl while bleeding out was an entirely different ordeal..

Music welled within his mind, transforming into an inaudible melody that conjured images of people long since gone and moments from what seemed like a lifetime ago. The heat of his wounds lay impassively against the chill of his skin, while sweat trickled down, etching track lines across his weathered face. His heartbeat reverberated, sending chills through his body. Anxiety gripped his chest and worry clouded his mind. Do was a man teetering on the brink of death, yet like many others unaware of their fate, he remained oblivious.

Guided by Nhat, he lowered himself into the corner, an effort that demanded an ounce of strength he could barely spare. As he settled, sweat glistened on his brow and his breathing grew labored. The wound throbbed, a sensation he recognized all too well from past injuries.

128

However, what he was feeling wasn't just pain; it was something far more dangerous—blood loss.

Seated against the pillar, his legs splayed out before him and his arms finally relaxing, Do breathed a sigh of relief as his body slackened. Glancing at Nhat, who stood waiting for instruction, he uttered reflexively, "My rifle."

Nhat gave him a perplexed look. He nodded towards his pack, placed beside hers, where his helmet lay and the imposing black instrument rested.

She regarded him uncertainly, and he reassured her, "Grip the barrel with one hand and the handle with the other. Don't worry, it won't hurt you if you bring it to me like that."

Watching her tentatively approach the weapon, Do again observed how small and frail she was. They were all victims of the evil men had wrought upon this place, he thought.

"That won't be necessary," intervened the voice that had joined them. "Nothing will harm you while I'm here." Do refocused his attention on the source—a fox, as Nhat had described. The creature that had guided her to safety stood nearby, emanating a reassuring light.

Do regarded it with wonder, believing what he saw yet struggling to comprehend the feelings stirred in its presence. Yearning to say something profound, something enlightening, he sat there with his mouth agape and eyes glazed. All that escaped his lips was a simple "Hello, fox."

"Hello, Do Duy," the fox nodded. "It's good to see you again."

Chapter Fifteen

The air was still. Neither insect nor beast dared disturb the silence that settled after a day of brutal violence. Do lay in the grass. Night had descended upon the town, and for now, both sides agreed that twelve hours of ceaseless conflict were enough. He didn't know what was happening or why such relentless fighting had broken out, but he knew one thing—it was his fault his brother Ca lay dead.

His brother's blood had dried upon his clothes. When the bullet struck, Do, only five years old, had tried his best to help his older sibling. Yet, the small hands of a child were futile against the wound gaping in Ca's chest. Five years older, his brother was no soldier but simply a protector trying to get his younger sibling to safety.

The soldiers had come. Their town's defenders went out to confront them. Guns unleashed their fire and noise and the whole town erupted into chaos. Do and Ca had been at school when the fighting began. Caught unawares, when the pair fled the grounds to take cover at home, they found themselves right in the middle of the mayhem.

Bullets ripped through buildings, bombs tore great chunks from the earth, and the clanking of armored warfare roared through their peaceful town. And the screams. Do would hear the echoes of those screams for the rest of his life.

Do couldn't comprehend what was happening; his brother understood but was hindered by the responsibility of being the older sibling. If circumstances had been different, Ca could have used that knowledge and escaped with his life. Perhaps Do would have been spared by the veil of ignorance that often protects a child. Yet, that alternate story would remain untold. Instead, he lay in the park's grass, surrounded by the silence that permeated the land.

Do turned to his brother lying on the ground, the moonlight reflecting off his cold, motionless face. His eyes stared up into the night sky, open and devoid of life. Years later, Do would wonder why he hadn't closed them, but in that moment, the five-year old boy gazed into the dead eyes of his older brother, hoping that they would flicker back to life, and he would be able to help him stagger home. Do's trembling fingers touched Ca's cheek, fear pulsing through his tiny heart.

"Anh," he whispered softly, "Anh hai, wake up." His hushed plea cut through the silent night, slicing the air like a knife. He stopped, freezing up in terror at the thought of being discovered. Waiting anxiously, he called out to his brother once more.

Not sensing any danger, Do sat up and began to shove at his brother desperately, a desperation that he wouldn't feel again until he became a soldier in a seemingly endless and brutal war. "We have to go," he urged, eyes darting frantically around, afraid that any commotion might draw gunfire.

"Come on, get up, I can help you." He pressed his forehead against his brother's, tears streaming down his face, an emotional dam breaking inside him that would soon dry up forever.

"I'm sorry. I'm sorry. Please. Wake up."

Do stayed there, weeping over Ca's lifeless body. His sobs echoed in the desolate night, lamenting his solitude, mourning the loss of his only sibling, and fearful over the uncertainty of his own fate and whether his end would come sooner rather than later.

His brother's body was stiff. His face bore an expression of eternal surprise, unaware of what had befallen him, oblivious to his own demise. Only Do knew what had happened. His mother and father remained unaware, but they would understand it when they saw his small form in the distance at dawn, wandering alone down that street with the morning glow illuminating his stained white shirt.

However, that was yet to come, a future Do couldn't fathom at that moment. For now, he stood in a field next to his dead brother, unsure of how or if he could find his way home.

Though moonlight lightly blanketed the town, it was still shrouded in darkness. The five-year-old Do had a habit of getting lost even during the daylight if he happened to lose sight of his big brother; how could he hope to find his way home alone in the dark? He glanced again at Ca— lifeless, cold, drained of all vitality.

Timidly, Do lifted himself from the ground. He looked around, half-ducked as he tried to examine the darkness around him without being spotted by anybody who might still be lurking nearby. The first of his senses that returned to him was sound. The world was so incredibly quiet that he learned the sound of silence itself could be heard.

As he took his first step, he was hit with sensory overload. The quiet rustling of the grass beneath his foot, soft, wet, and clumped together by the night's moisture and his brother's blood. The dry blood on his shirt had made it stiff, and it rubbed against his stomach and chest like cardboard. The smells of iron and gunpowder mingled in the air—a scent he would forever associate with his brother's demise. Amidst the encroaching darkness, pierced only by the moon and stars, fear lingered and a bitter taste of nausea rose in his mouth, the sour twinge of bile signaling—

Do retched and clutched his gut as he stood, bent over, expelling what little had remained in his stomach. At the last second, he managed to turn away from his brother; a gesture of respect, to not desecrate the body with his bile. A few more heaves and he was finished, tears streaming down his face, doubled over, and now openly sobbing. A lost boy in a lost world.

***

He had no idea what time it was. He had no idea where he was. He had no idea how to move, until fear reminded him.

Do had been standing there staring at his brother for some time when he at last heard a man say "est-ce que tu vas bien? parle-moi."

He didn't understand the words, but he knew that the language belonged to the enemy. Remembering what Ca always told him to do in times of danger, he ran.

Like a flash of lightning, Do vanished into the night, leaving behind one of the few people he would think about for the rest of his life.

The voice called after him again, "Arrêter! Je veux vous aider!"

Do only ran faster, fearing that the bad men would start shooting and kill him like they did his brother. His little legs didn't fail him. They carried his tiny body across the field and straight back to the school where he and his brother were when the city erupted in chaos.

Do stopped when he reached the building, the blood on his shirt wet again with the sweat dripping from his body. The metallic scent filled his nostrils once again and he remembered that his brother was dead. In the moments where he ran to the school, fear eclipsed all his other concerns in the world. He had forgotten, for just a moment, that Ca was dead.

Grief overwhelmed him once again.

Do found a small corner in the dark building to sit and cry. The place was empty and quiet, and he felt safe crying in its empty halls.

His chest heaved against his knees as Do sobbed, and he wrapped his arms around them. The tighter he squeezed, the safer he felt. Curled into a tiny little ball in the dark corner of the small school, the world seemed unable to harm him. It could not see him there, hidden in the shadows of a tiny town, in a country nobody in the world thought about until violence had descended upon them. He was safe.

The passing of time seemed cruel to the boy; how a minute could feel so long and how quickly so many of them could pass. Do had no idea just how much time had passed since everything began, or how long he had been at the school. It felt like a lifetime, but the darkness deepened, indicating that time was marching further still into the late hours. He sat, crying until he could cry no more. Hugging his knees, he stared out into the darkness around him, wondering when he should leave and if it was safe to go home.

His mind was flooded with fears, anxieties, and doubts. It was all too loud, overwhelming for anybody, especially a five-year-old boy. Instinctively, Do closed his eyes and focused on breathing.

Gradually his breathing steadied, his heartbeat slowed, and his muscles relaxed. Following his brother's advice for calming down, Do crossed his legs, placed his hands together in his lap, and closed his eyes. The day had been nothing but terror, lying in the field beside his dead brother while violence raged around him. The past few minutes he spent fleeing had jolted an already traumatized system, leaving Do feeling tense, angry, sad, confused, worried, and fearful, all at the same time.

The only thing he could do was breathe, just like Ca had taught him.

In the darkness, Do was transported back to the living room at home, meditating with his brother. "Count to four or five," the older boy had instructed him one day when the curious Do had asked what he was doing, "Breathe in and out through your nose."

Do couldn't do it at first, but Ca was always patient with him. He was never mean or harsh—beyond the standard teasing or scuffles between older and younger brothers, at least. Do would always remember how kind his big brother had been to him, and this memory was just one of many that he would recall later in life when speaking about him.

"Picture yourself sitting at the edge of your nostril like it's a large cliff. Feel the air that you're breathing in pass by." The older boy peeked to make sure that Do's eyes were closed, and he was pleased to see that they were. "How does the air feel to you?"

Do remembered sitting there trying it for the first time. The question made sense in that he understood the words, if not the meaning behind them.

"Like air?" Do asked inquisitively.

"No," his brother chuckled. "Imagine you're really on a cliff and the wind blows past you. How do you think it would feel?"

"Cold, I guess."

"Why cold?"

"Well, you told me to imagine standing in my nose like a big cliff. Maybe it's cold up there," Do replied innocently.

"Okay," Ca replied, amused. "Well, when you breathe out, how do you think that air feels?"

"What do you mean?"

"If the air is cold going into your nostril, how do you think it would feel going out?" The question was simple, but Do took some time to contemplate it. His brother remained as patient as ever, the two sitting cross-legged in their living room with only the sunlight between them. A happy moment. A warm moment. One never to be forgotten, yet one that would also be remembered all too sadly.

Some time passed. Do finally answered.

"Warm." He nodded with his eyes closed. "The air is warm."

"Good," his brother replied. "Now imagine that cold air going past you as you breathe in." He inhaled, and as he did so he counted. "One…two…three…four… now hold that breath." Ca paused and then exhaled slowly. "Now release, one…two…three…four…"

Do followed the instructions, imagining himself on the cliff with the cold air moving in one direction and the warm air in the other. He felt calm, at peace. He didn't know why his brother was doing this, but he was glad he interrupted him to learn.

134

"Your life will be full of both types of air, Duy," his brother used his given name. Do opened his eyes and looked at his sibling. The light shone on one side of the elder boy's face, casting the other in shadow.

"One day the air will be cool and pleasant, the other it may be warm and suffocating. Always remember to face them both the same way," Ca spoke with a gravity that Do had rarely seen.

"How do I do that?"

"By taking time to breathe and clear your mind," his brother said.

"That will help me?" Do asked.

"Maybe. It certainly wouldn't hurt you to try."

Do nodded. He didn't know exactly what his brother meant, but he committed it to memory. They both closed their eyes again and continued their breathing exercises.

"How do I know I'm doing it right?" he asked a moment later.

"When you're not asking me questions like that," his brother replied with a chuckle. It was an answer hidden in a riddle. Ca always talked to him like that.

He never would again.

The thought brought Do back to the present. He sat on that metaphorical cliff at the edge of his nostril, staring out into the darkness before him. He felt the thick, warm air surrounding him. He stood up and knew it was time to go.

Chapter Sixteen

Do stayed crouched by the school door. The night was still terribly quiet, the insects and other creatures maintaining their collective vow of silence since the violence had broken out. He sniffed the air and detected the scents of gunpowder, blood, and burning. The violence was still very real, and so was the danger.

He looked out over the town to get his bearings and, in a crouched stance, ran off in the direction he and Ca always took home.

The night was suffocating. The humidity and the lingering scent of gunpowder in the air combined and enveloped him like a wet towel scorched from putting out a fire. The panic, fear, and anxiety from before crept right back into his body. The meditation had only cleared his mind enough to find the courage to attempt the journey home.

His legs pumping, heart racing, and mind turning, there was nothing he could do to keep the demons of panic and fear at bay. He felt tears well up in his eyes but he quickly pushed them back, knowing that crying would only make things worse. He needed to be able to see.

The moon illuminated a path barely visible enough for him to see. Shadows surrounded him, and only the shapes of buildings rising out of the darkness told him he was probably going the right way. Even then, he only knew the general direction; he didn't know how exactly to get home.

The town's small buildings loomed larger in the night. Do saw them as mountains towering over him, carved from concrete and filled with people who dared not make a sound. If anybody saw him out there wandering the streets they didn't come to him, afraid of being blasted by a barrage of bullets or becoming the unwitting target of a bomb or artillery strike.

Do was suddenly reminded of his father, who always told him and his brother to stay away from the windows on nights when there were "talks." Their father always called these things "talks," discussions about the army coming to "take care" of everyone in town.

When he asked why, his father would always respond with a terse "just do what I say," and that was that. It was Ca who always explained things to him after the fact. Now that he was gone, who would fill that role? Who would lead him by the hand and patiently explain these things? Not his father, that was certain. His standard response to the child's questions was a smack to the head, leaving his ear throbbing and swollen. No, asking his father anything was always a gamble, and when mother's response was "ask your father," he always went to his big brother instead.

Do looked up at the ominous buildings, remembering all of this while scanning the empty windows. His dad was right; it was best to stay away from them.

A new horror seized Do's chest. His father. How would he react when Do came home without Ca? How hard would he be beaten for staining his school uniform?

Do stopped again. In the dead of night, in the middle of a deserted street, in a town currently under siege, all he could think about was what terror awaited him at home, completely oblivious to the ones that surrounded him in the darkness.

His brother dying was just the first in a long line of tragedies that awaited this poor child. An entire generation of children would experience this kind of loss, fear, and anger. However, only one among those countless children would share what he experienced next.

He squatted on the road, crying again. The latent fear of his father blended with the shock of watching his brother die on the ground before him. He had lain in a field for hours as bullets whizzed by and bombs exploded around him. It was too much, far too much for a five-year-old boy. He didn't know which choice was better; to die on this road at the hand of an unknown enemy, or to go home and be beaten to death by someone who was supposed to love him?

As he sat there crying, he didn't hear the soldiers creeping up from behind. They were trying not to alarm him so they could bring him to safety, but he had no way of knowing that. All he knew was that a hand grabbed his shoulder, and faster than he could think he jumped up and took off into the night once again, heart racing with fear, blood pulsing with anxiety, his mind filled with the images a child conjures up when he thinks there's something or someone out to kill him.

137

The voices called after him, but with the sound of his blood rushing through his ears he couldn't hear that they were speaking his language. They got a response, but not from him: the sound of guns and bombs once again tore through the night air, sending Do and everyone else in the town into a panic as they looked for a small corner of the world where they could hide and save their own lives.

Do's small legs pounded the dirt road. He could feel the dust kicking up behind him as he tore through the night, looking for something, anything that could show him the way home. All he could see, however, were shadows and the violent flashes of war raging around him.

Why is war so loud? he thought to himself, but he didn't have time to answer. As he neared an intersection in the road, he had to decide whether to go right, left, or straight. It was a split second decision that could affect the trajectory of his night. As fate would have it, this wasn't a night where personal choices would dictate one's destiny.

A jeep suddenly sped out in front of him, and in a panicked attempt to avoid running into it he slid into the ground, landing on his back, scraping his legs and sending dirt flying into his face. Through the dusty cloud, he saw a large gun mounted on top of the vehicle. Four figures jumped out shouted a phrase Do would learn the meaning of later: "Au feu!"

The figures before him unloaded their rifles at their targets behind him. He screamed, flattening himself against the dirt road as bullets tore through the air above him. The air around him grew hotter as the guns continued to roar. He clutched his ears and his screams of terror joined the cacophony.

Dirt flew into his mouth and stuck to the blood on his freshly scraped legs. Hot bits of metal rained down on him, searing his flesh as they bounced off his body. He caught glimpses of them in the moonlight and the flashes of their guns; little tube-like pieces of metal that popped out of the roaring weapons. As he watched this, one of the figures was struck by a bullet and fall backwards, splayed in the seat he was sitting in just a moment ago. Angry cries erupted from the other men, and they continued to fire at their unseen targets.

His gut said to lay there, but Do knew he couldn't. Eventually one of the sides would lose, and losing meant death. While Do wasn't yet certain that he wanted to live, he knew at least that he didn't want to die here. Clutching at his ears, he pushed himself along the ground with his legs. His scrapes reopened and new blood began to seep out, collecting dust and gunpowder as he crept along. He was getting nowhere without using his arms, but he didn't want to un-cup his ears.

Do desperately tried to take deep breaths like before, like Ca had taught him, but his face was smushed into the ground and the air was exploding above him. His panicked breathing turned into muffled screams, building up into an explosion of fury that propelled him forward and out of the fray in which he had suddenly found himself.

His arms flew down, pushed against the ground and lifted his whole body up and out of the madness that circled around him. One last push with his legs and he was up and out, running down the street and into the intersection. What had been a challenging decision just moments ago turned into a swift right turn for survival. He forgot about home and thought only about finding someplace quiet to hide and make it through the night.

The fighting continued in countless smaller skirmishes all around him. He sprinted down the street, moving from door to door, desperately checking for something, anything that was open. However, the only doors that weren't locked were barricaded from the inside. Desperation filled his heart; was there not one small corner in the world where he could find refuge?

Gunpowder and smoke filled the air once again, suffocating him. Do began to cough, snot dripping from his nose, and once again he started to cry. He sat against the nearest doorframe, clutching at his ears again, shutting his eyes and wishing that this would all just go away.

He curled into a ball, the only protection he could manage now. Though the air outside was plenty hot, Do's body shivered from the fear and adrenaline pounding against the inner walls of his veins. His mind was slipping away from him. In a moment he would be too far gone to attempt to get home. A bit longer than that and he would be too far gone to ever recover, a shell of the person he'd never have the opportunity to become, his fragile young mind so consumed by the horrors he'd witnessed that it couldn't comprehend the possibility of happiness. As he teetered on the precipice of total meltdown, he felt a different kind of warmth pushing past the night's oppressive heat, calming his tremors and easing his heart.

Do looked up, the icy grip of imminent death loosening its hold on his heart ever so slightly. A small ball of light hung in the air front of him. It glowed softly, illuminating the area around him in a gentle light. It was similar to daylight, but a bit more and a bit less; like the best part of the sun shining before him, easing his soul.

Do stared with wonder, completely entranced by the ball of light hanging impossibly before him. He looked around to see if anyone else was seeing what he was seeing, but only heard the ongoing sounds of bullets and bombs. Unnerved, he turned back to the ball of light.

It was about the size of a mango, but unlike the sweet fruit it was a perfect sphere. Do's mind drifted to his brother again, but instead of the pain of his loss, he felt the warmth of his memory. His mind filled with images of sunny afternoons together, the sounds of Ca's laugh and words of encouragement, the smell of meals they shared. It was as if a candle, poured from his brother's essence, had been lit inside of Do, illuminating everything inside that had grown dark and cold.

He looked at the light without fear or confusion. There was a lot he didn't know, but he knew that whatever this was, it wasn't here to hurt him.

"Are you not afraid?" The voice emanated from the light, falling over him like a blanket woven of music.

Do shook his head no. The light softened and its form began to ripple.

"Well, just so you're more comfortable, how about if I turn into this?" The light began to grow in size and extended in different directions. It wasn't an ugly process; rather, it seemed like the air itself changed to accommodate the new shape. It elongated and six different protrusions formed, four at the bottom and one at either end.

Do was so transfixed by the gentleness and beauty of the light that it took him a few moments to realize that it had taken the form of a dog. He giggled with delight when he saw what it had become, and the light moved closer and sat like a dog would, wagging its tail.

"Do you feel better now?" it asked, cocking its head to the side.

The child in Do was starting to resurface. He nodded vigorously, gazing at the light before him, still feeling its warmth and the love it had brought forth from within him.

140

"Good," the light softly responded. The being's brightness dimmed slightly before it continued. "Listen: we have to go now, Do. We have to get you home." The dog stood up on all fours, its lean body outstretched, ready to bound down the darkened streets that loomed ahead of them.

"Where are we going?" Do asked, still in a daze.

"Home," the dog said softly and authoritatively. "*Your* home."

Do's face dropped slightly. For just a moment, he thought he was going to be taken to a strange, far-off, magical place, away from all this. Instead, he was going back to a home where they didn't love him, where he would have to live without the one person who ever cared about him. His thoughts returned once more to Ca laying there in the field, all alone...

"Don't let your thoughts go there, Do. I need you to focus so I can guide you home," the dog said, standing with its front paws on the boy's chest as if it really were a lively animal ready to play. "And we have to leave right now; it's going to get far more dangerous here. Do you understand?"

Do let out a gentle sigh that ended with a little sob. He wiped his tears and nodded, mumbling a weak "Okay." The word was soft, broken-hearted, and stifled by his sinuses from crying so much, but the dog understood it came from the boy's heart.

"Good. It's going to be okay. For now, follow me and do as I tell you. We won't have a better chance than we do right now to get you home safely."

Do nodded and rubbed his eyes as the dog got back down on all fours. It looked up at the boy and nodded. "Ready, Do?"

"Ready."

The two set off into the night, the boy free of worry or fear. After all, what more could this world possibly take from him?

Chapter Seventeen

Sergeant Do Duy remembered everything as soon as he saw the light take the shape of a dog. The memory had been locked away in the recesses of his mind, buried underneath the rubble of years of death, chaos, and dismay. He should have remembered it when he heard the girl's story, but he was so transfixed with the demon hunting her that he could scarcely think of anything else, including the guiding light that brought him safely home the night his brother was killed by communist forces who were supposed to be fighting the French.

It was strange to think of his brother now, in this way, after not having thought about him for so long. He felt his throat tighten with emotion, but he maintained his composure; there was still so much to do right now. All the same, he saw his brother's smile, felt his warm touch, and tasted the mangos they used to eat together when they were kids.

"It was a quick walk home." The light, having returned to the shape of a fox, began to speak again once it saw the recognition in Do's eyes. "Do you remember what you talked about when we walked that night?"

"I do," Do said, nodding with a finality that told The Fox that he was willing to do what was necessary. "We talked about the responsibility of life," Do continued, his voice tinged with solemnity. Do knew what it meant. The Fox, that was the light, knew what it meant. It was the reason why Do was here and his brother was not.

Do sighed heavily with relief, bearing the weight of responsibility that was now his. He was glad that all of this would soon be over. He couldn't imagine much of a life for himself after the war ended, win or lose. It was the eve of retreat, and while he knew that soon his life would come to an end—a thought he welcomed after decades of violence and bloodshed—he wondered if he could complete this one last act. Some might call it an act of redemption, but for him, it was atonement for the lives he had taken in order to extend his own.

"I'm confident we could make it to the coast," he said after some time, "were it not for that *thing* that was chasing her."

"The Evil."

He and The Fox both turned to face Nhat, who was sitting on her legs, kneeling as if in a temple. They regarded her in awe, for all that she had been through and all that she would go through still. They waited to see what the little girl had to say.

"That's what I call it," she whispered as she wrung her fingers in her hand.

"Why is it chasing you?" Do asked.

"I don't know," she said quietly. "Mama, Papa, and Anh were gone. Then after I got the package from my uncle, it came out of the dark for me."

"The dark?" Do asked.

She nodded. "It was hiding in the dark in Papa's office. I think it was living there."

Silence settled over the room. *Of course it came from the darkness,* Do thought.

"How do we kill it?" Do asked, a practical question befitting a soldier.

"You can't," The Fox said, looking directly at Do. "It is already dead."

"It's dead?" asked Nhat, her chin resting on her arms atop her knees. Her demeanor was calm, almost subdued. Do admired her resilience. He thought of himself as a child, after he'd made it home that night. The things he saw were too horrific to comprehend, so he didn't. He shoved them down into places where they couldn't resurface, and there they remained until now. He wondered if she was doing the same thing.

"It is indeed," The Fox said, "but to be more precise, it never lived."

Nhat looked up at him and Do regarded the light with a look of confusion.

"The Evil, as you call it, is the sum of all things that have died in this war and weren't supposed to. It is the culmination of all the carnage and death that has been wrought in this country in the name of politics. Every soul taken, every life cut short, every light snuffed out resides in that creature, and it seeks only to gain one thing: vengeance."

"Vengeance?" Nhat asked.

"Revenge," answered Do.

Nhat looked at him, thinking about what he had just said.

"Revenge for what?" she asked, turning back to The Fox.

The Fox moved its head as if looking down at the ground, though it appeared to Do that it was glancing towards him. It was difficult to discern the focus of its pupilless eyes.

"For getting dragged into a conflict they didn't want to be a part of. For having their lives taken away when they weren't ready." The Fox then looked up at them. "You see, all these lives that have been taken, including those involved in the fighting, were meant for so much more."

Do felt himself settle. He looked at Nhat, her legs crossed, staring at The Fox. The same being that guided him home decades ago and told him of the sacrifice that was to come. His thoughts were drifting away to what his life could have been when The Fox spoke again.

"War is not a part of the natural order, of that… 'divine' purpose. No one is ever meant to fight in war, to die in it. Some would reason that it's just human nature, that it's a part of your 'purpose,' but it isn't. Interpersonal conflicts and even violence are inevitable, this is true, but large-scale murder in the name of political diplomacy is not a natural way for individuals to leave this world."

The Fox looked at Nhat and added, "People weren't meant to fight and die for someone else to have money and power."

Do looked at the girl and she nodded, understanding the addition.

The Fox continued. "The greatest tragedy is the sense of community that is torn apart when such wide-scale conflicts arise. Wars are often portrayed as an effort to benefit the nation or ease the suffering of its citizens, yet they are carried out at the expense of harming others. Concepts like community and sovereignty are manipulated to trick people into killing and being killed by other people who have been equally misled. It is an inherently unnatural act."

The Fox glanced off into the distance before returning its gaze to them and continuing.

"It is those same spirits, who died in such a terrible manner well before fulfilling their purpose, that make up what you, Nhat, have so aptly named, 'The Evil.' The creature is more than just death itself; it is the embodiment of mankind's defiance of the natural order." The Fox then turned directly to Do, adding, "It does not matter which side you are on. Whether you take a life or surrender your own, your death and life have

144

been snatched away from you. They're sacrificed to an unnatural cause, in turn breeding an unnatural existence."

Silence filled the room. Do's breathing had steadied; in fact he was very relaxed in the presence of the light. Nhat, too, had finally been able to relax a bit. Would The Fox be able to guide them both safely? He was about to speak up, but was cut off by sweet voice of a life that had been invariably changed by the unnatural conflict in which he was an active participant.

"Do you know?"

"Know what?" The Fox asked in reply.

"Do you know what all those people were supposed to be?"

Do was surprised by the question. He had wondered that himself from time to time, what he would have been if his brother hadn't died, or if the war hadn't gone on his entire life. What he would be if he wasn't a Sergeant for the ARVN, if he wasn't a killer. What his brother would have been if he had survived and fought in the war too, or what he would have been if there was never a war at all.

"Yes. I do," The Fox answered. Looking intently at Nhat, Do saw himself in her. Would she share his fate? Or would she have a chance to live the kind of life she was meant to?

"What were they supposed to be?" Her innocence, Do thought, had not been driven from her completely.

"Poets. Doctors. Teachers. Mothers. Fathers. Friends. Caretakers. Some mechanics. Some writers. Others who just laid around all day and did nothing. Most would have had families. Some were to be perfectly content without. Lovers, all of them; of life, of food, of books, of music, anything and everything. I can see their lives, all before me, never to be." The Fox paused for a moment. "There is only one that I can save."

"The girl," Do interjected.

"No. Yours. You can handle saving the girl. The life I am meant to save, that I am here to bear responsibility for, is yours."

Do's expressionless face did little to hide his incredulity. "I'm already too far gone," he said flatly. The liquor Nhat found earlier had given him an edge he'd kept in check up until now.

"No, actually," The Fox stood up. "Your life has yet to begin." It walked over to an empty spot in the room. It stood on its hind legs and began to melt into the floor, its light stretching out to reach every corner

145

of the room. "This is just an example; I can't show you what is to be. For that would be an irredeemable act, and even a force like myself must answer to the power you call 'God.'"

The light continued to pour all over the room, spreading color and light to the dark, abandoned, desolate place they had stumbled upon. Eventually, after everything had been illuminated and restored to its former glory, the scene changed to show a family sitting down for dinner.

"There's nothing special here," The Fox's voice was all around them now. "No thrilling spectacle to behold. What you see is a family gathering for dinner, a mundane moment in an ordinary life. Yet despite this apparent normalcy, the woman at the table, gazing contentedly at her children, is currently on her way to one of the ships you yourself intend to reach." The voice paused, allowing Nhat and Do to absorb the scene before them. "She's a little girl, like you, Nhat, but her trajectory is already clearly charted. The path that the two of you walk, however, grows more clouded with each step you take. I'm here to remedy that."

Do studied the family at the table once more. A tableau of peace, tranquility, and routine. Luxuries none had had in their war-torn country for quite some time. He wondered if the country could ever have it again. Could anyone gather at the table like that, eating and enjoying each other's company? The idea rattled him to his damaged core. Would *he* ever be able to do that, after all he had seen and done? Just sit down and…and *eat*?

"Just like that, huh?" Do asked, thinking about his own past and the bleak future it pointed towards, marred by the damage done to him and all the people of his nation.

"I understand the situation you're in," The Fox gently replied. The light and color slowly faded from the room, the scene before them melting and receding back into the ball of light that was the original form of this being. It floated before them for a moment, casting its typical warm glow on them once again, before approaching Nhat in the shape of The Fox. It spoke peacefully, but Do was still unable to fathom the thought of a normal life awaiting him.

"It is indeed possible for both of you to live meaningful lives after this. It's why I'm here. To make sure that The Evil that chases you doesn't succeed in exacting revenge on two people it hates the most," The Fox sat on the floor, letting what it said sink in.

146

"It hates me?" squeaked Nhat, her little finger pointing to her own chest, confusion and fear in her voice. "Why?"

"Me I understand, but why the girl?" Do asked.

"It is an amalgam of all those who died in this war and saw what they could have been. For you, it's simple; you're an instrument of the unnatural process that sent them to where they are now. For Nhat," it turned its gaze to her, "they hate the potential her life still holds, the possibilities they could never have now. They want you suffer in the way they have suffered." The Fox paused—Do thought he sensed hesitation—before it spoke once again. "Which is why it took your family."

The moment The Fox said it, a flash of images burst into Do's mind. Things he had never seen before, people he didn't know. A young boy, still sleeping, being lifted out of his bed and devoured whole. Familiar claws gripping and crushing the father's body, his mouth frozen shut and a look of terror in his eyes as his son's bare feet inched down the monster's throat in front of him. Nhat in her bed, sound asleep, a multitude of blankets piled on top of her by her terrified mother before she ran to another room, leading the creature away from her daughter. Her locking the door in the office, sacrificing herself to trap the beast, sealing her fate.

He looked at Nhat only to see heartache and confusion etched on the girl's face. Her gentle eyes told him she had not seen what he'd seen. Why was he shown what had happened to her family?

"It killed my family?" she whimpered.

"I'm sorry, little one, but it's true," The Fox said, "and it won't stop hunting you until its hatred has erased any chance for your family to live the life they were all deprived of."

Nhat shot up and ran to Do, tears streaming down her face. He winced as she slammed into his wounded body, but held her in a tight embrace all the same. Two orphans, separated by twenty some odd years and connected by spilt blood. He held her tight until her tears subsided and her sobs turned into gentle huffs of deep breath.

"Tell me what to do," he said to The Fox.

***

"Okay," Do concluded after their lengthy discussion. "It'll take some careful work, but we can make it. Are you sure?"

147

"My light is fading. Once your enemy has taken over this country, the last vestiges of hope will fade, and I with it," The Fox sighed.

"So, you'll just...die?" Do asked.

"No. I will return to the void, rest a while, and come back as starlight."

"Aren't you starlight now?"

"Goodness, no," The Fox chuckled gently. "Although I may appear as such, I am a living force much like you and Nhat. However, my life force is tied to something you would perceive as a higher being. We are all a part of the same life force, some of us more aware of it than others."

Do looked at Nhat sleeping on the floor next to him. She had finally succumbed to the fear, exhaustion and grief of the past few hours and could remain awake no longer. "So, you give your life for ours. Then what?"

"You live."

In his mind, it still seemed impossible. In his heart the prospect was somehow terrifying, and in his soul it was nothing more than the scattered pieces of an idea torn apart long ago. Even with The Fox telling him all this, he just could not see it ever happening. A life? How ?After all he had seen and done?

He pushed it out of his mind for now. "I can do it; I can get us out of here. Are you sure you can defeat that thing?"

"Light always prevails over darkness. Even you humans have subdued the night with your torches. Trust me—I can stop The Evil."

"And if you can't?" Do's uncertainty lingered. The predicament he found himself in was its own kind of hell, and navigating it was a different kind of torture. His previous enemies had been humans like him, and that he could handle. Throw an entire battalion at him, and he would either defeat it or die. This, however, was something beyond him. The stakes were higher; it wasn't just about his own life anymore, but also about saving the life of this girl. It was about creating a life beyond mere survival—one that didn't involve taking the lives of others to sustain his own. Not having to sleep in the rain. Not having to hold your breath, praying that you weren't seen. Not having to sleep next to a dead friend because moving would risk your own life. Not having to relive the terrible

148

things you've done in your head over and over and over again. Being able to truly have a life.

To defeat the demon and live a normal life afterwards—both seemed nearly impossible.

Do looked at The Fox, at the girl, and then down at his own hands. "Do we have to leave now?"

The Fox gently shook its head. "No. My presence is enough to keep it away. For now, you two must rest." Shifting its form, it settled on the floor like a normal animal, its hind legs tucked underneath its body and its front paws stretched out. It held its head erect, like an animal on alert after taking a rest. Do marveled at the regal being, just like he had when he was a kid. It blanketed him with a calm that allowed him to breathe. He pictured himself again, on the edge of his nostril, the wind blowing back and forth. He remembered his brother and his life before all this—the fact that he even had a life.

"How long can you stay with us?" Do asked, once again trying to reassure himself that it was okay to rest, unable to reconcile the peace he felt in his heart with the other thoughts running through his mind.

"Until it comes for you," said The Fox. Though lacking eyes, its presence seemed to bore into his. Invading the portals that led to its very soul.

"Do you think we can make it to the coast before that happens?" Do dreaded the thought of encountering the demon again. It was truly a horror to behold in and of itself. Now that he understood the true nature of the monster, he was terrified at what he might have to face. Himself included.

"I wouldn't be prepared to sacrifice my essence if that were not the case," The Fox said, laying its head down. Do wondered if it was weary. "Even though I will be gone once all hope is lost, I still very much like to live as long as I can." It made a noise resembling a sigh. "Truth be told, this happens a lot to my kind. We live, we thrive, and when war breaks out, we are at last summoned to live as a star and recuperate for eons before being returning again in this form. Our kind are very sensitive; after enduring such trauma, it takes an eternity to heal."

Do stared, but before he could say anything The Fox spoke again, "You should take care to rest, Do. While I'm not long for this world, you very well might be."

149

Silence hung in the room.

Do thought about the path before him. He had a life to live. He didn't know how he would do that, but for the sake of the little girl who appeared in his life, and for the sacrifice of this being he wasn't entirely certain about, a little voice inside his head suggested that perhaps, it was worth a try.

The Fox had fallen silent, its glow softening. *Even they rest*, he mused.

He looked around the now-dim room. He tried to lie down, but the pain surging through his shoulder persuaded him instead to sit back up and lean against a nearby wall. It wouldn't be the best night's sleep, but it would do.

The Fox faded until it was a barely recognizable shape, a distant glow in the night. Do closed his eyes, and his weariness carried him off with little trouble. He dreamt of soft lights floating in the air, filling his heart with warmth. The lights drifted on, changing shape into things that he recognized as life—glimpses, traces, moments of it. Scenes of happiness, of family, of enjoying food, music, dancing, loving. Breathing peacefully on a beach as the wind passed over him and the sun gently shone on his face. Sitting at a table with a family, smiling. Driving a motorcycle in the countryside of a distant land. Smoking a cigarette with a hot cup of coffee. These moments presented themselves to him for just a brief amount of time, but they filled his heart with something he hadn't felt in a long time.

Hope.

Chapter Eighteen

Do woke up just in time to see The Fox fade from view as rays of sunlight began to creep through the cracks and crevices of their shelter. His shoulder throbbed dully from the combined pain of yesterday's wound and sleeping sitting up. Though he ached all over, he carried the warmth of everything he saw in his heart. The potential joy that his life still held, and the anxiety of their present situation hanging around his neck like a weight, woke him up.

A real life. It was possible, he thought, but was it plausible?

Nhat remained motionless. He looked at her and thought of what kind of life she would have without her family. Maybe she would have to stay with him. Maybe *he* could be her family. The thought vanished as quickly as it came when a voice filled the room.

"The sun is out, don't waste it. Leave now." The Fox spoke to them from beyond their senses.

Do nodded, understanding that they had to make use of the daylight as much as possible. He shoved himself up to his feet, wincing but not groaning. He had learned to suffer in silence long ago. His body ached all over, screaming for relief. He found the bottle of liquor that they used to sterilize his wound. There wasn't enough for a decent drink, but he downed it all the same, hoping that it would at least loosen his tight muscles. He stepped gingerly to the girl and bent down, his legs burning, and gently shook her awake.

"Em," he pressed her shoulder, "It's time to go." He stood up, knowing that she wouldn't be long. There was no time to waste; they both knew this. His experience as a soldier and her terror over the last few days had left them tormented—him from the war, and her from the terror it created.

There wasn't any food left in the old restaurant, but Do wondered if there was still running water. He found the old sink in the kitchen, where piles of dishes used to be washed daily. To his surprise, when he turned on the tap, water still flowed. Do shut it off and returned to the main area of the room for his pack. They would need to leave soon, but he had time at least to boil some water for their canteens. Rummaging through his things, he took out the necessary items: a pot, a portable stove, and a gas canister. Fortunately, he hadn't needed to use it yet. He could make a fire easily enough in the field if needed, saving the gas for true emergencies. He went to work setting it up as Nhat finally stirred and sat up to watch him.

"What are you doing?" she asked, still sleepy.

"Boiling some water for us to drink and to take on our journey," he said, twisting the canister to the tube, "You should get up and get ready, we have to leave soon. I'll boil some for us to drink now, and while that cools I'll boil more for us to take."

Nhat rubbed her eyes and walked over to her pack. She opened it, retrieved a bottle, and brought it over to him. "We can drink this now and refill it so we don't have to wait." She handed the bottle over to Do and returned to her bag, pulling out packs of dried food.

Do watched her, once again impressed by the girl's resourcefulness. When he was her age, he wasn't nearly this thoughtful or knowledgeable about such things. How much of her childhood did she lose because of this calamity? Was there any of it left to salvage after this?

Do stood up with his pot and said "You go ahead—eat and drink. I'll have what's left, and we can refill the water after it's done."

She nodded and continued to take things out. He watched her a moment longer before leaving to fill up his pot.

***

They sat and ate while the water boiled. Nhat had offered him the dry fish and took the dried beef for herself. They each had a cup of the powdered milk she brought, and he offered her a browning banana that he had in his pack. He passed her a can of rations, but after a tentative nibble of what was supposed to be turkey loaf, she politely refused and passed the can back to him.

"Yeah," he said, taking a bite, "the Americans don't like it much either. That's why they give it to us." He chewed on it, looking at the can, "You get used to it." He took a small sip of water and passed the bottle back to her. Nhat accepted and drank greedily. She wiped her mouth and handed it back again.

"You can finish it," she said quietly.

Do looked at her and drained the bottle. The water he was boiling was more than enough to refill it and make some coffee for himself. He had just enough left in his pack for a cup, as well as the sock he'd been using as a filter over the years. He didn't really need it, but in his dreams the previous night he saw himself enjoying a cup in the future, and it resonated with him in a way. Not quite hopeful, but something like it.

"Do you think we're going to make it?" Nhat asked, as if she had somehow read his mind. "To the coast?"

"We're going to try our best," Do said, speaking candidly.

"And if we don't get there?" she pressed on, looking up from where she was folding the plastic that previously held the dried beef.

"We meet our fate," Do replied. He never had much interaction with children. He didn't know how to get down to their level.

"What's fate?" she predictably asked.

Do shifted, crossing his legs and wincing internally at the pain in his shoulder. "Fate," he began, "is what we're all meant for. Some people call it destiny. Others say it's the thing you're put on this Earth to do, but for me it just means the end. No matter what it is. Sometimes it leads to another journey, sometimes it doesn't. Whatever your fate may be, there's nothing you can do to stop it. The only thing you can do is meet it like an old friend."

"An old friend? Like give it a hug?"

Do laughed, for the first time in a long time. "Well you can't hug fate, but you have the right idea. You welcome fate with open arms and it can't hurt you."

"What if you die?" Nhat asked, tepidly.

"Think about it this way; if you die, is there anything you can do about it?"

Nhat thought about what he said for some time, staring at the floor ahead of her before finally shaking her head.

"Exactly," said Do, turning off the stove to let the boiling water cool. "There's nothing you can do when death comes. Same if it's your fate. So why worry?"

"But won't you be sad if you're not alive?" Her eyes were filled with wonderous curiosity and worry.

153

"I don't know, em, truly. I don't think anyone knows until they're dead how they feel about it." He shrugged, "After all, no one's come back to tell any of us, have they?"

"I'm never going to see any of them again." Nhat looked down, toying absently with the sheet of plastic.

"In this lifetime, no." Do said. He didn't want to sugar coat it. He didn't know if she'd seen what he had when The Fox told them The Evil had killed her family, though he certainly hoped she hadn't. It was something on top of an ever-growing pile of things he wished he could forget.

"I only have their things now," she pulled her bag close, "to remember them by." She sighed and added, "I only took things. I didn't think about taking a picture."

"You'll always remember them," he said without hesitation, "I haven't seen my brother since I was very small—younger than you, even—and I can still see his face when I close my eyes and think about him." He reached out to touch her on the shoulder, ignoring the pain of his wound. "It will be the same for you. Just remember the good times. Learn to meditate. In time you will be able to hear their voices when you think they've long since faded." He smiled at her, but it went unnoticed. Nhat hugged her bag and began, once again, to cry.

Do removed his hand, finished the last of the old water, and refilled the bottle from his pot. There was nothing for him to do but let her weep. It was the one thing that was natural in all of this calamity, crying. What else can you do when your family and friends are all dying around you while your country is being ripped to pieces?

Steam rose from the bottle as it grew warm to the touch. He set it to the side and packed his things, letting the little girl cry with the bag of trinkets that was all that remained of her family. He wished he could do more to comfort her, but right now the best he could do was to get them the hell out of the city and country.

He sat while the water cooled, letting the girl cry her heart out. Once they were on the move out in the city there would be no time for that—only running. They had to make the most of the daylight while they had it. He worried about what the night would bring, when the monster could move freely again. Would The Fox be able to stop it? Would they be able to escape the carnage the thing represented? He didn't know. The only thing he knew was that it was time to leave.

Nhat cried. He sat and accepted the prolonged rest. The sun rose, signaling the end of their time in the country they called home.

***

A thick air of oppression hung over the streets. For a city that had just been under siege, things were unnaturally quiet. The entirety of the capital seemed to be holding its breath, waiting for something they thought would never come.

It was foolish to think they would win; Do saw that now. There was nothing to do now but accept that they had lost and, in that, lost their country to a system that would forever tell them what to do, think, and feel. Do gazed around, looking for the enemy, but also taking in his homeland one last time.

What he saw was the same thing he'd always seen since this started: pain. The deserted morning streets meant millions of people hiding in their homes, worrying, scared, terrified, holding their loved ones on the floor praying that a bullet, bomb, or battalion wouldn't come crashing through their home and kill them all. This was a moment in war that history books don't typically mention. The silence.

"Let's go," Do said, gripping Nhat with one hand and his rifle's grip in the other.

They set off in the fresh dawn, the only sound in their immediate surroundings the pounding of their feet on concrete. In the distance Do could hear the military vehicles he had learned to keep an ear out for. The north had come full force. There was no sound of resistance, not a hint of his allies taking a stand against their enemy. A heaviness settled in Do's heart. They had truly lost.

The two ducked low and ran alongside the buildings. They were going to have to move fast and get off the streets. Nhat was a little girl with a south soldier. While she would not be harmed, as the child of an enemy combatant (they wouldn't care enough to get Do's story beyond what they would see) she would likely be sent to a reeducation center and he would be publicly tortured and executed.

155

They would have to move quickly and quietly, stifling the discomforts they faced while they fled The War and The Evil created by it. If their bodies hurt, they would have to push. If they felt hunger, they would have to fast. If they felt like giving up, they would have to stand and push on. There would be no rest until they made it to the coast, on to a boat, and out of this country. He wondered if he could do it with his wound…and if Nhat could do it at all.

The light was soft and comforting on their skin. In an hour's time it would be bright and full, unforgivingly beating down on them until dusk.

"Come, this way," Do whispered and let go of Nhat's hand, running to the opposite corner of the street. He picked up his rifle, scanning the area they had just left. He saw the restaurant where they had slept in the distance, its shell forlorn against the outskirts of the city, wishing its temporary inhabitants a fond and sorrowful farewell. Do thanked the building with a light bow of his head and quickly turned to scan the distance ahead of him. He saw a small trail of smoke in the distance. He knew it would be coming from school they found Nhat in and where they had fought The Evil.

Do scanned behind him one more time, assessing his surroundings the way all good soldiers did when they needed to move. The smoke of the school was a pale grey, and the sound of the enemy vehicles was well enough away that he didn't have to worry about being seen on foot out here. He looked to the east, where the sun was coming from, and then to the southeast at what would be their destination. Knowing there would be patrols throughout the day and check points all over, he decided that their best bet would be to stay off the roads. As tough as it was and as hard as it was going to be, they would have to travel through the jungle.

Nhat reached his side, her scurrying silent, and she landed neatly next to him. He looked down at her as she focused on her surroundings, clutching at the too-large bag.

"Come on, let's go," he said, and they hurried down the street, heading southeast towards a place where even the brave feared to go.

***

The jungle. Those words were enough to elicit wonder and excitement in anyone studying geography or reading tales about a fictional adventurer. To a soldier, however, it meant certain death. Whether you took an enemy's life or they managed to get the drop on you, going into the jungle meant someone was going to die. It was especially true in this country, and it was most especially true at night.

While he wanted to be gentle with the child, Do couldn't help but rush her as they navigated the jungle leading to the coast. He didn't want to be here when night fell, and he certainly didn't want to face The Evil in an area where nothing was predictable.

The girl was having trouble. She had never walked in the thick brush like this. She explained to him that while she had gone camping many times, her family had always stuck to the trails when hiking.

He considered this and thought about taking the riverbanks to the coast, but he was worried about patrols and decided against it. While it was difficult and the small girl moved slowly in the rough terrain, he knew they would have a better chance of evading detection if they stayed in the wildly unpredictable jungle. The irony wasn't lost on him; in fact, he was all too aware of the perils that faced them between the jungle and the coast, day and night, life and death. He knew the dangers, but it was worth the risk. The hazards of the jungle could be mitigated, the risk of facing a squad of enemy soldiers could not. The only question left in his mind was whether or not The Fox could deliver when the time came. For now, the two of them had to simply press on.

Four hours had passed since they escaped the city into the jungles surrounding their once beautiful capital. Getting out was easy; Nhat had already traveled a great distance on her own when they found her in the suburbs, and the rest of the city was only sparsely guarded. They had encountered a few patrols, but they waited, biding their time and moving when it was safe to do so.

The girl seldom made a noise. She was good at moving evasively and taking orders. It seemed the only thing she wasn't good at was being a child. In her eyes Do saw an adult doing all that she could to survive. The carefree spirit and youthful spark was absent. She was a child of war now. He knew the look all too well, having worn it himself for most of his life.

He stopped and wiped the sweat from his brow, taking a sip from the canteen he had filled up at the river when they first entered the jungle. He saved the boiled water for her; he could handle the river parasites. He turned back to see her stumble over a clump of roots. She didn't complain,

157

but he could tell that the unpredictable terrain of the jungle was taking its toll on her. She was tired.

"I would pick you up and carry you on my back, but with my shoulder the way it is, neither of us would last upright for very long."

The girl said nothing, nodding and watching her footing. She was determined, but all the same, he could see the weariness in her little frame. Her black hair stuck to her like a wet piece of paper, her clothes soaked all the way through, and her little cheeks flush with exhaustion.

"Stop," he said. He walked over and took his pack off, relieving his shoulder, and placing it against a tree with his rifle. "Take off your pack, you need some water."

Nhat replied silently, slouching off her pack, pulling out the bottle and sitting on the ground to drink. She didn't chug it like he feared but took thoughtful sips. *This girl's been on her own for a while* he thought to himself.

He looked around, not wanting to sit because he knew that would make it harder to get up again. The girl needed the break; he could give her fifteen minutes before they had to move on. It was almost noon. Once the sun crested, they would only have seven or so hours of precious daylight. He wanted to close the gap between them and the coast much more than they realistically could. It probably wasn't going to happen, but they had to try.

The air was stifling. How many times had he slept in the jungle, full gear, empty stomach, waiting for something to happen? For someone to kill? He looked around. The animals of the jungle paid no mind to the war that was raging around them. Only when the fight came here did they stop and flee. Otherwise, life went on around them, without a care for their political rhetoric and strife.

"How much further?" Nhat's voice came out small and tired. He looked down to see her staring straight up at him, her brown eyes dark and unnerving. He could see the exhaustion in their depths, laced with fear and longing.

"I'm not going to lie to you Em, we have a long way to go."

She looked down again, taking another small sip and replying with a weak "Okay." She sat staring for a moment before looking up at him again. "Can I sit for just a little bit longer?"

158

"I can give you fifteen more minutes," he said, checking his watch. The time could be spared if she was able to move more quickly afterwards. If she slowed down after the rest, he would have to limit their breaks in the future.

"Thank you," she said and laid against her pack, closing her eyes.

"That pack must be really heavy," Do said. "Why don't you just leave it?"

"I can't" she said, opening her eyes and looking at him, "It's all I have left."

"You're willing to risk your life for those things?"

"No." she shook her head slightly, "It's just that I need them. I only have four copies and I don't want to lose anything just in case."

"Four copies of what?" Do asked, confused at the statement.

She turned around and pulled her backpack forward, unzipping one of the pouches and pulling out a small bundle of papers. She handed it to him. "This one isn't wrapped. The others I wrapped in tape and plastic to protect them from water. I don't want to lose any of them if I don't have to."

Do took the papers from her, amazed again at the young girl's wisdom. He unfolded the papers, reading everything over and understanding immediately why they were so important.

He had seen plans like this before, heard about them many times from family, friends, and his fellow soldiers. Do was never one to make plans like this. He was the only one left in his core family unit, and he didn't plan on surviving the war anyway.

"My uncle sent them," Nhat said, still gazing up at him. "I need them in order to leave."

Do nodded, carefully folding the documents and handing them back. "Okay," he said, "put that back in the pack."

She took the papers and carefully returned them exactly where she'd retrieved them from and looked to him, waiting for further instructions.

"Your uncle is a smart man." He placed his hands on his hips and looked around. "If we're going to make it by tomorrow morning, we have to move faster. I can take your pack for a little bit as long as I don't tire out my shoulder, but you need to be prepared to pick it up quickly and run if we get into trouble. Do you understand?"

159

She nodded.

"OK. You have ten more minutes or so. Lay down and relax your muscles, then we're going to walk quickly for four more hours."

Nhat nodded and did as she was told. She lay her head on her backpack and stretched out her legs, letting them recover from the toll the jungle took on her.

Do removed a cigarette from his front pocket and lit it. There was no risk of the light or smoke being spotted among the trees during the day. He thought about her travel documents and was filled with increased urgency. The girl had family out there that could take care of her. He had to make sure she made it.

He inhaled the nicotine and stared out at the jungle before him. The sun shone through the trees. The birds sang their songs while other animals in the distance made their own noises. He could hear the river if he really focused on it. It was a beautiful day, but he and the girl were in no position to enjoy it.

He leaned up against a tree, enjoying his cigarette and listening to the familiar sounds of the jungle. The pack of Marlboros he found on a dead solider had lasted him quite a while. He knew the end was coming and wanted to enjoy the good cigarettes for as long as he could. He was down to three in the pack and, God willing, he would smoke the last ones on a boat taking the girl to safety. Fate had allowed him at least to smoke this one in peace. It wasn't until he was about to throw it out that he heard another familiar noise, one that stood out against the idle sounds of the jungle.

Quickly he ducked down, shaking off his pack and readying his rifle, ignoring the searing pain in his shoulder. The girl shot up but he placed a finger in front of his lips and motioned for her to lay back down. She quietly and quickly obeyed, terror filling her eyes. He looked around slowly, his rifle trained on what was in front of him. Everything was green and brown and glowing in the fierce sunlight.

Do steadied his breath, listening for the sound of boots in the jungle. He spotted an enemy soldier in the distance, walking slowly, rifle at the ready, looking for a target that Do knew to be the two of them. The soldier was twenty-five meters away, but Do could see him clearly. The enemy had not seen him yet, and Do wanted to keep it that way.

160

He laid his rifle gently on the ground and unsheathed his combat knife, a K-Bar given to him by an American soldier years ago. He looked at Nhat and again motioned for her to be quiet. He knew that she would obey—the terror in her eyes told him so.

Carefully and methodically, he crept on all fours towards the other solider. Each movement was silent, each inch a precise calculation. Do felt his fingers grip the knife tightly in his fist as he crawled towards his target.

The enemy soldier let out a sigh and mumbled something derogatory that Do could hear faintly through the brush. He had not been seen; the soldier was looking for them but had gotten impatient, and in war, impatience is costly. This soldier, Do knew, was about to get himself killed.

Crawling until he was within five meters of the other man, Do kept his breath steady and silent. The years of meditation served him well. There in the jungle, with the enemy before him, he moved stealthily, making no noise on the jungle floor.

The soldier shuffled quietly, his boots shifting as he turned to continue the search for those he was hunting. Do could see the man's boots in front of him, dirty from trekking through the forest. He waited until he saw the heels to make his move.

The jungle betrayed neither man. Caring not for what was going to happen, the birds sang their songs and the mammals chittered away. Mosquitos buzzed all around him, looking for exposed skin to feed upon, but Do retained his military bearing. If a snake came up and bit him, he would not have called out. His mind was clear, his heart was hard, and his body did only what he willed it to do. Do adjusted the grip of his knife and waited for the soldier to turn his back.

Minutes didn't matter during these moments; everything came down to seconds. In the two seconds it took for the enemy soldier to turn away, Do had his hand over the man's mouth and his blade deep within his throat.

Do felt no pain in his wounded shoulder. He felt only the brief struggle of his enemy against the blade in his throat.

Slipping it out slowly, Do felt the blood of his enemy slide down the handle of the blade and onto his hands. He could smell the iron in it and felt the man's body grow weaker with each gurgle that emanated from his throat's wound.

161

Sergeant Do Duy led the man down slowly, taking care not to make a noise, as this scout's unit was no doubt nearby. He could feel the warmth leave the soldier's body. The limbs relaxed and the body grew heavier as he lowered him to the jungle floor. Do stayed a while, watching the life leave the man's eyes. Pupils dilated, lips turned blue, and a steady stream of blood down the front of his uniform, Do knew that he was dead. Another life taken; another dream deferred.

Do wiped the blade clean on the dead man's uniform and took his canteen. He searched the man for anything of use and found only personal effects that he couldn't be bothered with.

Looking around for anybody that might have followed him, Do stayed low to the ground and returned to the girl.

***

He wouldn't meet Nhat's gaze, though he could feel her staring at the blood. Instead, he opened the canteen he'd secured and sniffed its contents. The water was clean, and the canteen was full. He recapped it and used the river water in his own canteen to wash his hands. The warm blood came off with ease, and he wiped his hand dry on his trousers. Not one to waste the water, Do finished off his canteen and put it back in his pack, along with the one full of clean water.

"Let's go," he said, placing his pack on his back and picking up his rifle.

Nhat didn't hesitate. Wordlessly, she put on her pack and they set off into the jungle at a low run. Do didn't tell her to stay low, but noticed that she tried to match his speed and stance. *Quick learner* he thought, and the two didn't say another word until the sun began to set and they could go no further.

162

Chapter Nineteen

The warm glow of dusk fell gently on their resting limbs. They finished off the food from Nhat's pack, and she even took some of the turkey loaf Do offered her when he opened up a new ration can. They drank their fill of water, careful to leave some for the next day. The sun felt gentle on their faces, but anxiety grew in their hearts as the light slowly faded away.

Night was coming, and The Fox had not yet arrived. Neither had The Evil, but Do was getting concerned about which one might show up first.

Neither of them had spoken much when they stopped to eat. While he knew that she knew that he had killed someone and it made her uncomfortable, he had to break the silence.

"Does it always show up at the same time?" he asked, scooping the last of the turkey loaf out of the can.

"No," she said gently. "He always comes when I need him to." She looked off at the setting sun. "Always right on time. Like you."

"What do you mean, like me?" he asked. They began returning things to their packs now that they were done eating.

"When I was at the school…" She hesitated a moment. "It was about to eat me." She pulled her knees to her chest and rested her chin on them. "It had me by the backpack but I fell and ran away. I hid, but it found me again." She closed her eyes and sighed. "It had me in its claws. I was about this close to its teeth—" she held her hands up at a distance of about fifteen centimeters. "—that's when you and the other soldiers came. You all saved me just in time. Like The Fox."

Do leaned back against the tree, feeling the stiffness in his shoulder. He touched his hand to it and found, thankfully, that it wasn't hot. Heat meant infection, and even though it hurt like hell he was relieved. He looked at Nhat, who was still looking at him.

"Did it hurt you?" he wondered out loud, "When you were that close to its teeth?"

163

"No, the only thing that hurt was when I fell down again." She crossed her legs and placed her hands between them. "I was more worried about my bag. It had it, but when you came to save me I was able to find it. I was scared that I'd lost my papers."

"Well, lucky for you that's the only thing that happened."

"I'm scared about losing them again though. That even if we live, I won't have them because of *it* and I won't be able to go to my uncle." She looked up at him with sadness in her eyes. "I don't have anyone anymore."

Do nodded and felt a weight of sympathy for her. He knew how she felt. He was the last of his family, like her. He'd learned how to manage the hurt over the years though; she was barely beginning to grasp what had happened.

"Well, I will do my best to protect you and get you there. The rest is up to The Fox, I suppose. If he lives up to his agreement and helps us the rest of the way."

Nhat nodded and the two fell into silence again. Do was thinking of what they would do if The Evil showed up again, while Nhat sat silently staring at her hands.

"Light," Nhat said after some time. "Light is the only thing it's afraid of." She looked at him with certainty. "If we can make it to the morning again, we'll be ok."

Do nodded and gave this some grave consideration. If they managed to escape The Evil and walked through the night, they would be able to make it to the coast. He didn't know what they would find there, but it was the only chance they had. He could manage a small boat or skiff; he was certain he could make it to the escaping Navy. Their big ships were still out there, rescuing anyone who could make it. Again, all they could do was try. He was about to tell her this when they both heard it.

Nhat's head shot up while Do grabbed his rifle and instinctively went into a kneeling position. His rifle trained at a point in the distant darkness. The growl was still some ways away; Do remembered the intensity of it. He guessed it was about 250 meters or so away and heading towards them. He lowered his rifle and went quickly for his pack.

"I have a strong flashlight in here," he said as he dug, "will that work against it?"

164

Nhat shot up. "Yes, it will." She went for her backpack, "I have one too."

Each of them rummaged around and produced their flashlights. Do took out a roll of duct tape that he used for quick weapon fixes.

"Here," he grabbed her hand and wrapped her fingers tight around her flashlight. "I'm going to tape it to you, so you don't drop it." He wrapped the grey tape around her multiple times, going over her thumb and wrist to make sure it was secure. He clicked the light on and illuminated the area around them. "Here." He grabbed her backpack and secured it as well, wrapping tape through the straps and around her waist. "This way you won't lose it."

When he was done with her, he grabbed his own flashlight and tapped it to the barrel of his rifle, taking care to wrap it multiple times to protect it from the heat of exploding rounds. He switched it on, placed his rifle on the ground, secured his pack, and picked up the rifle again. He stood up, helped Nhat to her feet, and said only one word to her:

"Run."

***

The growl of The Evil grew more insistent. With every meter they ran in the encroaching darkness, the monster seemed to keep pace with them. Neither stopped, fearing for their lives, but while they grew tired, The Evil did not—and would not. With Nhat directly in front of him, Do could feel the creature, the manifestation of hate and anger of the war's victims, behind him. Eventually it would catch him, and then the girl. He had to decide whether to keep running, or to stop and engage.

"Keep. Going. As. Much. Can." His breathing was labored, his shoulder on fire, and his legs screamed at him to stop. "Okay?" he managed to huff out.

"Okay!" Nhat shouted. Do could see her little legs pumping furiously in the small amount of light that emanated from her flashlight. She held her arm out in front of her so she could see. The dwindling twilight mixed with the yellow glow of the flashlights gave them just enough visibility to see where they were going without falling flat on their faces. When it was finally gone, they would be alone in the dark. He thought of The Fox and its light, how they could use it right now. Would

165

it live up to its word and show up right when they needed it as Nhat explained? Or has its light gone out, leaving them alone to face The Evil that he, in some part, had helped to create?

Darkness closed in around them, the twilight hour fading and the erratic movement of their flashlights offering little more than glimpses of spaces they could use as footing. While Do was adept at hunting, traveling, eating, and killing in the dark, sprinting was another story—especially with a young child to consider. Do glanced at the fading horizon, its purple hue already disappearing. Then he looked behind him and recognized the giant pair of yellow eyes he had seen last night. They moved steadily in the darkness, not bobbing up and down like a natural creature's would. They stayed level in the darkness, drawing closer to them, centimeter by centimeter.

Do was out of ideas. In fact, he'd had none to begin with. They wouldn't be able to continue like this forever; eventually, they would have to stop and face it. He worried about losing track of Nhat in the darkness, as well. There was no plan, only the instinct to confront evil whenever he was destined to meet it. They had to stop. They had to confront this *evil* head-on, with or without the Fox. This was their fate.

"Nhat. I'm-going-to-count-to-ten," he stammered out between breaths, "On-ten. Stop. Running. Okay?"

Nhat turned her head. Even in this darkness he could see the worry and doubt on her face, but she nodded. "Okay!" she shouted, her voice labored and her breathing heavy. Do was right—they weren't going to last much longer like this. They needed to face this thing if they were going to have a chance at escaping it and the country. He wiped the sweat from his forehead and began to shout his countdown.

"One!"

His feet pounded the jungle floor, preparing for a full stop that would shift his weight down and back so he could engage the creature with his rifle.

"Two!"

The pain in his shoulder reminded him that he was for now, still alive.

"Three!"

Trees and brush cracked behind him. It was catching up.

"Four!"

Searing pain tore through his lungs.

"Five!"

Safety off. Round chambered. Hopefully the rifle wouldn't –

"Six!"

– jam or they were really –

"Seven!"

screwed.

"Eight!"

Get your head on straight Sergeant –

"Nine!"

– we've got work to do.

"Ten!"

Do shifted his weight and pivoted, spinning into a hundred- and eighty-degree turn. He saw Nhat had begun to slow down but didn't completely stop. She didn't know how to control her body like that just yet. He shouted into the darkness behind him, "Stand behind me and shine your light at where I'm pointing!"

He hoisted his rifle up, the beam of light from the flashlight cutting through the dark and illuminating the trees and brush of the jungle. Each lead or vine looked somehow fake, shining in the light against the pitch-black backdrop of the jungle. He heard rapid footsteps behind him before a light flashed on over his shoulder. He breathed a sigh of relief; he hadn't lost her.

There wasn't a sound to be heard in the jungle other than the pair's labored breathing. Do took notice, as the normal sounds of nocturnal animals, birds and insects were absent. That only happened after a heavy battle—the silence never came before. The creatures of the forest knew something was amiss, and they dared not make themselves known to whatever it was that brought this ominous weariness, this feeling of dismay, that which seasoned soldiers recognized as impending death.

In the darkness, Do cautiously checked his rifle, sliding back the bolt receiver to ensure it was loaded without making a sound. His fingers then moved to his knife, unclipping it and ensuring it was ready for use in close combat. Two feeble beams of light pierced the darkness, revealing only a fraction of their surroundings. The ominous yellow eyes that had trailed them had vanished. Do took a moment to steady his breath, then reached out to reassure himself of Nhat's presence. He gently patted the top of her head before returning his left hand to the barrel of his weapon, bracing himself for whatever came next.

Being hunted was a strange feeling. When it was by enemy soldiers, Do rationalized that he was doing the same to them, a violent dance of survival. However, this time, he felt the primal instincts of thousands of years of human evolution coursing through his veins. His heart raced with terror, his mind urging him to flee, yet his weary spirit rooted him to the ground, preparing for what could very well be the last fight of his life.

Silence. Not a single sound escaped from the darkness before him. Do knew it was out there waiting, but for what?

"Turn off your light." Do said, switching off his own.

"What?!" Nhat asked, confused at the command.

"Turn it off, but keep your hand on the switch. Turn it back on as soon as I start shooting. Then we're going to run, stop and do it again. Do you understand?"

He couldn't see her response, but after a quick moment her light was extinguished, and they were plunged into total darkness.

Silence prevailed. Do relaxed his muscles but kept his hand on the light, his left arm extended on the barrel, ready to flick it back on as soon as the beast revealed itself. Do knew it had been waiting for its element. It was waiting for the shadow.

The yellow eyes emerged from the void five meters in front of him. The Evil had crept up to them quickly, silently, and was ready to pounce on him, devouring his body and soul and adding it to the collection of human misery that comprised its very being.

Do turned the light on, illuminating the monster's fleshy grin. It smiled at him with its perfect human teeth and the mottled tan and pink flesh crawled around its face, singeing where the light shone on it. The Evil didn't mind it; in fact, it seemed to be enjoying the pain before the kill. Do looked into its eyes and saw the misery and torment that had plagued his country for decades. It was mesmerizing, in a horrific sense.

While Do hesitated, Nhat brought her light up to the monster's face as well. The combined power of both lights was too much for the creature, causing it to pull back, snarling and gnashing its teeth in her direction. Do snapped back to reality and unloaded his weapon into The Evil's face. Bits of teeth, flesh, and one of the creature's eyes flew into the night air. Do held the trigger of his automatic weapon and unleashed a devastating display of firepower. With the two beams of light in its face and hot metal ripping it apart, The Evil roared with all the rage it could muster and staggered backward. When Do felt the empty click of his weapon, he grabbed Nhat's hand and sprinted into the darkness.

Looking back, Do saw that the creature remained stationary, its one good eye glowing in the darkness as it roared in agony. He released Nhat's hand and switched off his light, immediately reaching out for her again. They ran in the dark, putting distance between themselves and The Evil writhing in the shadows.

When he estimated that they'd run about two hundred meters, he stopped and told Nhat to turn her light back on. He got into a kneeling position and reloaded his rifle, ejecting the empty magazine and slapping a full one into place. He chambered the first round smoothly, as he had done thousands of times before, switched on the flashlight and waited.

They both struggled to catch their breath, sweat running down their faces. They hadn't gone far; they knew it would come again soon. Do wondered when the hell The Fox would show up. If this wasn't when they needed it the most, he could barely imagine the terror they had yet to face before it would come.

The jungle fell silent once again, and he knew that they were still in danger. He had six magazines left, including the one he'd just loaded, two grenades, and his knife. If it took all of that to get to the coast, so be it. There wouldn't be much he could do if it got back up to chase them after all of that. *Where is that damn Fox?* he thought.

"Turn off your light." The two beams clicked off at the same time. This time, however, The Evil came for them immediately, its lone eye rushing towards him in the dark faster than before.

"Turn it on!" He flicked the light back on, but The Evil managed to knock him down just as the beam seared its torso. Do plunged his rifle barrel, the light still firmly attached, into The Evil's mid-section. He pulled the trigger and held it down, unloading thirty rounds into the creature's abdomen. It roared in pain, and he pushed it back, adrenaline kicking in and masking the pain in his wounded shoulder. Nhat screamed and shone her light on the creature's face, causing it to roar again and gnash its teeth at her. Do didn't hesitate this time; he pulled out a grenade, yanked out the pin, and shoved it into the creature's mouth. He grabbed Nhat by the hand and took off once again into the dark of night.

***

They stopped after another two hundred meters. His lungs burned. Nhat collapsed on all fours, choking and gasping for air. They left their lights on as protection, knowing that the creature would be on them again soon. He heard the grenade explode and flesh spraying the trees around them. He hoped that would be the end of it, but he had seen the monster get back up after so much worse before. It had at least bought him enough time to orient himself.

He took out his compass and held it under his flashlight. They were heading south. Lucky for them; he was worried that they got turned around in the chaos. He readjusted himself and faced southeast. Gasping for breath, he told Nhat, "We're going to do that again, but this time we're not going to stop running for a long time. I don't have enough ammo to do this all night and we can't sprint like this forever, either." He put the compass in his pocket and slapped another magazine into the rifle. *Five left,* he thought as he steadied the rifle at his hip, directing the beam in front of him. He looked over at Nhat who was still on all fours, staring at the ground.

"Are you OK, Em?" His heartbeat was calming down, but his lungs were still angry with him.

"No," she gasped, "I can't breathe."

"It's okay," he said, "Just take deep breaths. We've got a few seconds. It won't come with the lights on, we'll be okay."

Just as Do finished his sentence, Nhat screamed as her little body was lifted high into the air. The Evil stood, its face mutilated and torso ripped in half, the left side dangling, dragging its arm and claws uselessly on the ground. Its one good eye was fixed on Do, who lifted his rifle and shot it square in the sickly yellow orb.

The creature roared and dropped Nhat, who hit the ground with a hard thud. The Evil stood, its one good arm clutching at its face. The bear-like creature, standing on two legs, emitted a blood-curdling shriek into the suffocating darkness.

Do ran to Nhat; she was unconscious. The impact of the fall had knocked her out. He kept his rifle trained on the beast, pulling her away from it. The creature started thrashing its arm about, blindly searching for a target.

170

He pulled with all its might, dragging the girl who was now dead weight. *Wake up* he thought as he leveled his rifle and fired three rounds at the creature. It roared again, tearing a nearby tree to splinters as it flailed with its one good arm.

Finally, Do got a good grip on her backpack and was able to drag her away, firing intermittently at the wounded creature. With the beast in this state, they could make great progress towards the coast, but not until the girl woke up.

With no other option, he let go of Nhat and loaded a fresh magazine. *Four left.*

Once again, he lifted his rifle into the air and fired a volley of shots at the creature. It stepped back, roaring. Encouraged, he stepped closer and shot a three round burst at it, aiming where its heart should be.

All that The Evil could do was roar and stagger back. It hit a tree and fell, writhing on the ground. To Do, it looked like a colossal skinned bear laying on its back, dying on the jungle floor. Taking advantage of the situation, Do continued to fire at it, walking closer and emptying the magazine into its head.

It stopped moving.

Do kept his rifle trained on the beast. He wasn't going to fall for this again. He shone the light on its flesh and waited for it to burn, but nothing happened. He nudged its body with the barrel of his rifle. Nothing. Finally, he took out his knife, stabbed it into the creature's face and pulled it out. Nothing. Not even any blood on the blade when he pulled it out. For all intents and purposes, The Evil appeared to be "dead."

Do didn't believe it. He removed the mag and inserted a fresh one. *Three left.*

He fired a single shot into its eye socket. It remained unmoving.

He stepped away, his rifle still trained on it, inching backwards towards the girl. His eyes still fixed on the creature, he knelt next to Nhat and gave her a shake, hoping that she would stir. She remained still.

Do wiped his brow, gazing at the illuminated corpse of The Evil as it lay enshrouded in shadow and flickering acritical light. Did he kill it? *I certainly hope so*, he thought.

The silence of the jungle, however, gave him no reason to believe it was dead. He remained on alert, shaking the girl intermittently so they could get the hell out of there.

171

Finally she stirred, groaning and rising up on her knees to rub her face. He took her flashlight, still secured to her hand, and examined her face with it. Her left side was red and swollen. She would be quite bruised, but that would be the worst of her injuries.

"Can you move?" he asked.

Nhat looked around in a daze and nodded. Her eyes were hazy and unfocused, but she was up and moving at least.

"Come on," he said. "We have to go while it's down."

Nhat looked over at The Evil and stared, her little body tense but traces of hopeful relief on her face. "Is it dead?" she asked.

"It looks like it, but we can't relax until we get the hell out of this country." He looked at her. "Can you run?"

Nhat turned to him, her arm with the flashlight taped to it dangling awkwardly at her side. "Can we walk for a little bit?"

He took out his compass and oriented himself before putting it away again to check the time. It was just past eight in the evening. They still had a long way to go, but they had to make good use of however much time they'd get while the monster was down. "We can walk until eight-thirty. After that we'll jog for a little bit and then walk some more, back and forth like that. Can you do that?"

Nhat looked up at him with her swollen face. "Yes, I can do that," her voice sweet and relaxed. She appeared relieved, believing that The Evil was dead. He would keep his pessimism to himself. The girl needed a win. So did he, in fact.

"Okay, come on," he said, lifting his rifle. "No sleeping tonight. We have to make it to the coast by sunrise."

She nodded, lifting her hand with the light still attached.

"We'll take that off when the sun comes up," he added, and they set off into the night.

As he walked, he thought about what had just happened. He wondered if The Evil, like The Fox, was close to death as the war was coming to an end. He allowed himself to relax his tense body, but his mind stayed alert to all that was around him.

As they walked, Do heard something he didn't expect: the sounds of the jungle were slowly returning, and even the mosquitos began to approach them again. He took out his repellant and sprayed both himself

172

and Nhat from head to toe. Life had returned to the jungle. It gave him hope. All he had to do now was stay focused.

The soldier in him didn't permit him to relax, but the sounds of life did give him a tiny bit of hope that they would make it after all. They had each already survived the worst days of their life so far; what was a few more hours?

So much for The Fox, he thought as he tapped his watch, and they began to run towards whatever waited for them at sunrise.

Chapter Twenty

There were still two more hours of darkness left, but Do heard something that made him forget the possibility of a demon chasing them: waves, crashing in the distance. The sound of water receding, foam hissing on the sand, and the hum of the ocean lulling people into a calm that only the tropics could provide. He sniffed the air and smelled the salt. Tuning his ears, he heard horns in the distance. The Navy. The coast. They had made it.

Judging by the sound, it was still quite a distance away, but as soon as daylight broke they wouldn't have to worry about that. They could make it. They could *actually* make it.

He sped up, his eyes having adjusted to the darkness since their flashlights burned out an hour ago. Clutching Nhat's hand in his, with his rifle in the other, he pressed on, determined to make it. He was so focused on their goal that he didn't notice how worn out Nhat had become. He didn't notice that his wounded shoulder was burning from overexertion. He didn't notice that the reason he could hear the coast at all was because the jungle creatures had once again fallen silent.

"Come on. We're almost there. Can you make it?" Do urged, his voice strained with determination

Nhat didn't have a chance to answer before Do's legs gave out from under him. At first, he thought he had finally collapsed from exhaustion, but when he heard Nhat scream and felt something grip his legs, he knew he had relaxed too soon. His soldier's edge dulled by hope and the prospect of survival.

The Evil tightened its grip on Do's leg, dragging him closer with terrifying strength. Do managed to grasp his rifle, unleashing a barrage of shots into the darkness. Amidst the flashes of gunfire, he caught glimpses of The Evil—transformed into something more sinister than the bear-like beast he had fought before. It now possessed an elongated body, lined with multiple pairs of insectile legs, a spindly tail that thrashed wildly behind it, and a vaguely serpent-like head. The giant pair of sickly yellow eyes was gone, replaced now with six smaller blood-red orbs glowering at him menacingly in the dark. About the only feature that remained from before was its set of human teeth, though now it was a snake's tongue licking them as it pulled Do forward.

Do ejected the now-empty magazine and forced a new one in as he struggled to break free of the insect-like claws.

Two left.

He raised his rifle again, firing into The Evil's face as Nhat's bloodcurdling scream pierced the darkness. Every shot hit its target, but no flesh exploded from its face. Instead, each round was absorbed, sinking into its body, and The Evil grinned wider, licking its lipless grin. It pulled him slowly, savoring the fear that now coursed through his veins. It was toying with him. It knew: it had him, and there was no escape.

Do reached for another magazine, but before he could grab it he was raised into the air five meters and slammed into the ground. The force of impact stunned him, knocking the air out of his lungs and sending a raw surge of electrical pain through his nerves. In all his time in combat he had never felt such agony.

With a sickening satisfaction, The Evil pulled Do close and loomed over him, running its serpent tongue over his face. It was cold, wet, and the odor was putrid beyond description, even surpassing the stench of death. Do heard Nhat screaming in the background, but there was nothing he could do. The Evil had him and now he was going to become another soul bound within this wretched creature's body. Do had always thought of his inevitable death as a welcome escape, but this fate was beyond anything he had ever feared.

The Evil stood on its multitude of legs, towering above them at a height of at least twelve meters. Its red eyes blazed with a sinister passion. Do could tell the creature delighted in his impending demise. For The Evil, this was a long-delayed over the man who made its existence that much more miserable than it already was.

As Do closed his eyes, he silently asked Nhat for forgiveness as he prepared himself for death. The Evil unhinged its grotesque jaw so as to consume him whole. With a single forceful motion, it thrust Do into its gaping maw, engulfing him entirely.

Nhat's scream echoed through the jungle, a chilling cry unheard by any human soul.

175

***

Cold crept over Do. He knew that The Evil had eaten him, yet still he felt. He waited for the crunch that would end his life, the quick and terrible pain that would send him into shock before his world went black and he found out whether it was oblivion that awaited him or the eternal consequences of the life he had lived.

He waited, but it never came.

Do opened his eyes, but saw nothing in the pitch blackness that enveloped him. Even in the jungle at night, he could at least make out shapes around him with the help of the moonlight, but here inside the beast, he could see nothing. He felt as if he were floating, a sensation he found unsettling. He reached out for something, anything he could use to orient himself, but he felt nothing. He was in an empty void.

"Em."

Do straightened up, trying in vain to locate the source of the voice. "Who's there?"

"It's me, Em. It's Ca."

Do tensed up immediately, his heart filled with sorrow, his mind with terrible memories, and his soul with a pain that he had not felt for thirty years. "Anh?"

"That's right," the voice of his big brother said. "It's me. Your brother."

"Where are you, Anh?" Do said, choking up, tears already streaming down his face.

"I'm here. But you can't see me."

"Anh!"

"Calm down, em. Remember the cliff on your nose? Go to the cliff."

Do's tears flowed freely, his sobs wracking his chest as he shut his eyes tight. "Are you alive?"

"No." his brother's voice said, solemn and distant. "I died a long time ago."

"Why are you here? Where are you?" Do managed to get the words out between sobs.

"I'm here. In this prison. I've been here since I've died."

176

"Are you not at peace?" Do asked, remembering the teachings from temple in his youth. He had hoped that his brother had reincarnated somewhere far away from home, where he could not be harmed.

"No, none of us here are," Ca explained. "That's why you have to kill this thing that has imprisoned us. It takes our souls and traps us here, makes us part of itself. We don't know how long we've been here, we don't know how long we'll stay, but we know that we can be freed. Some have been freed before, released when you thought you had killed the monster. But as more people die out there, it has more souls to strengthen itself again."

Do could only continue to weep.

"Em, you have to kill it."

"How? It keeps coming back and getting stronger, I don't know how to put it down for good." Do gasped for breath. "Brother, please, let me see your face. I'm sorry. I'm sorry that I got you killed."

He felt a warmth wrap around his body. A love that he had not felt since the day his brother died. It was familiar, caring, and it smelled of the fruit they would cut up and eat together.

"We have no faces here brother, but we're here."

Do continued to cry. He was reunited with his brother, but just barely so. "Forgive me, anh, forgive me for all I've done."

"There will be time for that em, when it is your time. I will come for you and we will spend some time together before the unification."

"Before the what?"

Ca laughed gently, filling Do's mind with images of his brother and warming his heart even though it wanted to break.

"You will learn about that later. For now, you must free us."

Do took a deep breath and let out the remainder of his grief. "Tell me what I have to do."

"Follow the light."

At first, he thought he was imagining the brightness building up in the distance. Do blinked a few times and rubbed his eyes. He still floated in the void, but was very much aware of his own body. He focused and saw the light building up in the distance.

"I will see you again, little brother. For now, free us and survive."

Before Do could respond, the void was filled with light. What had been inky blackness a moment ago was now a blinding slivery-white.

177

He threw his hands in front of his face and closed his eyes. Suddenly, he felt a force of speed that shook his entire body. He called out to his brother but couldn't hear himself over the rushing air that enveloped him. If his brother said anything else to him, he didn't hear it. He was in a tunnel shooting straight out. The light was so bright that it blinded him even with his eyes closed. His body shot up like a rocket, and then everything went dark again.

***

The first thing he felt was his body hitting the ground with a thud. Pain radiated from his shoulder once again. He heard Nhat screaming for him and then felt her little hands on his body.

"Anh! Anh! Can you hear me?"

"What happened? Where am I?"

"Look!" she screamed with awe and wonder.

Do looked up and saw The Evil writing in pain. A bright light was emanating from it. He could see it clearly now. It had six legs with claws at the end, a lizard's tail, and the head of a serpent with six eyes. Its flesh was the same as before, crawling all over in different sickly shades. Shades that he now knew to be human flesh—that of the people that it had consumed, writhing from the souls trapped within.

It was standing on its two hind legs and clawing at its abdomen with its other appendages, its tail thrashing wildly. It staggered back, burning from within.

Do immediately knew what it was, and Nhat confirmed it.

"The Fox! I told you it would come when you needed it most."

He looked at Nhat, who stared at what was in front of her in awe. She had no fear; The Fox was here as promised, giving everything it had left to fend off The Evil.

Straining to stand up, Nhat rushed to support him as he rose to his feet. His rifle lay on the ground in front of him. He picked it up and backed away, extending his arm so that Nhat would follow as they retreated from The Evil.

The two marveled at what was happening. The Evil was being consumed from within, The Fox attacking it at its very core. Pieces of flesh began to fall off, and the beast screamed again and again. Do knew that

178

the pieces of flesh falling off were souls escaping. He hoped that Ca was one of them. They stood for a moment longer in wonder until beams of light began shooting out from The Evil. Its red eyes dimmed and its limbs went limp, no longer fighting what was consuming it.

At last, the monster collapsed backward and the light slowly faded from its core. Do and Nhat crept closer, eager to see The Fox again, but stopped when they heard its voice.

"It's not dead. I've given all I have to stop it for a while, but it will rise again, and it will come for you. Run. Don't waste this time. Go."

"Thank you!" Nhat shouted, jumping up, acting for once like the little girl she was.

"What about you?" Do called out.

"I will shine down on you from above. Now go!" The Fox emerged from The Evil's ruined body and laid on top of it, its light slowly fading. "We will see each other again, away from all this madness. Live your lives and don't look back."

It laid its head down and its light slowly went out. The glow around them faded and before it went dark again, it simply said: "Run."

***

Do and Nhat ran with renewed vigor, fully ignoring the pain in their burning legs and their screaming lungs and their aching hearts. They ran as fast as they could, dodging brush, with branches whipping their faces and cut their arms as they flew by. Do's rifle was strapped to his back, slapping against his shoulder, while Nhat's backpack pounded her legs unrelentingly. Each of them ran for their lives. Each of them understanding that life could be theirs, and with the coast so close, they just had to keep running.

Do glanced at his watch as he ran, catching glimpses of the time in what little moonlight remained in the sky. One hour until dawn. They could do it. They had to. The Fox had fulfilled its promise and bought them time. If they could just survive until dawn they would make it. Getting to the Navy was another problem they could handle once The Evil wasn't a concern. Do ran harder, his resolve never stronger. He got to feel his brother's presence one last time, he knew there was something after this life; now he just had to make this one count.

The two eventually slowed, but they kept a steady pace. The sounds of waves grew stronger with each step. The Pacific Ocean was right there, he could smell it. They just had to keep running.

They ran for forty minutes straight. Do checked his watch again. Dawn would be coming in twenty minutes. They could walk the rest of the way once the sun came up. Once the sun came up, they would be halfway free.

He let hope fill up his heart again.

"Em, are you ok?"

Nhat nodded furiously, her hair shaking in the air and the excitement in her body showing through her determination. He smiled, laughing at the child whom he found alone and dejected two nights ago. *She might have a life yet*, he thought.

He wanted to tell her to slow down and walk the rest of the way when he felt the air grow cold. For a split second he thought it was a runner's high, but he knew better. The Fox was right; it was coming after them again. He didn't have to tell Nhat—she tensed up and began to run faster, having also felt the chill that The Evil brought everywhere it went. Even in the steaming jungle he got goose bumps. He tightened his rifle strap and ran faster.

They felt the pounding of the ground through their feet. The Evil was now clambering after them, tearing at whatever stood between itself and what it had been hunting all this time.

Do again glanced at his watch—fifteen minutes. They could do this. They could make it. They weren't going to give up here. Even if he had to give his life for hers, she was going to make it. Dying to save her wasn't giving up in his mind; it was still succeeding if she could reach her family in France. He would take her as far as he could.

"Faster, Em!" he called out. "The sun's almost out, we can make it!"

"Ok, Anh," she called out and looked back at him, "I believe in you!"

He smiled, for the first time in a long time. He knew what he had to do. Thirteen minutes until the first rays of dawn, give or take a few. Too close. He had to give Nhat her chance.

"Keep going. Don't stop when it gets close. I'm going to slow it down, but for now keep running."

180

She didn't nod or otherwise motion to signal that she'd heard, but he hoped she would continue on when the time came.

The air was growing colder by the second, the rumbling below their feet more intense each time they hit the ground. *Five minutes,* he thought, *it's going to be on us in five minutes.* He unslung his rifle and made sure it was loaded. He had two magazines left, one grenade, and his knife. He was going to make each of them count.

Do didn't need to look back to know it was coming for them; in fact, he wouldn't look back until he felt its breath on the back of his neck. He was ready to take it on one last time, to buy them enough time for the sun to come up and obliterate it for good, or at least send it running back into the shadows so they could flee. Whether it was he or the beast that lived or died, Nhat was going to get out, and he was fine with that.

He checked his watch again. *Twelve minutes to sunrise, four for the beast, two magazines, one grenade.* His heart pumped faster, not from running but from the anticipation of this final battle.

His breath materialized in the air before him, the moment growing closer as they edged toward the coast. He pumped his legs faster, hoping to gain valuable seconds against this monster that feasted on the terror the people of his country felt during this calamity. The war had brought this monster, but its end didn't kill it; it made it grow.

Eleven minutes to sunrise, three for the beast, two magazines, one grenade.

He entertained the idea of stopping now and engaging it here while she ran, but abandoned it immediately when Nhat screamed. "Look!"

Do was brought back to the moment at hand. In the shadows of predawn, he saw the trees thin out and give way to open air and clear ground.

The coast.

They made it. A mere one hundred meters and they were there. They had done it. Now he just had to keep her alive.

Ten minutes to sunrise, two for the beast, two magazines, one grenade. He could do it.

"Faster, Em!" he cried out, "You can do it!"

The Evil roared in response. Do stole a look back and saw the creature three hundred meters away. This was it. This was the final battle. It didn't matter what happened to him, Nhat was going to make it. The

181

sun would rise on her swimming out to the Navy; she was going to be okay.

Nine minutes to sunrise, one for the beast, two magazines, one grenade.

In that moment, Do thought of everyone he had lost, of those who never really got to live, of those whose lives were forever changed, and of the whole country that would suffer for years to come. He laughed to himself; there was nothing to do but to meet fate the way he told Nhat—with open arms.

Eight minutes to sunrise.

***

Do breathed a sigh of relief when Nhat broke out of the jungle and onto the beach. An excited smile on her face, she turned around just in time to see him dive forward, roll onto his back, and train his rifle on The Evil as it bounded towards him. He switched to semi-auto and fired carefully, making sure every shot landed. They all hit the beast square in the face, with three bursting several of its eyes.

Last magazine.

He reloaded and took off towards the beach, yelling at Nhat to make for the water. Nhat screamed at the sight of The Evil again and ran for her life toward the beach. Do sprinted off to the left, luring the beast away from her. He dove again, ignoring the pain in his heavily damaged shoulder, sand flying into his eyes and mouth.

Trees cracked and broke as The Evil emerged from the jungle, towering over Do like a two-story house. It flexed its appendages and stalked toward him, eager to devour him again. With The Fox gone there would be no intervention, and Do would become another of the countless souls which comprised its essence. Even in the face of this threat, if he could just last long enough for the sun to come out, the souls of all who died in this war, including his brother's and his own, would be released and able to rest in peace. Dead or alive, Do was going to make sure they were set free.

He took off down the beach, running diagonally so that he could see Nhat heading for the water. The gigantic, insect-like beast stomped towards him, catching up much more quickly than he anticipated. Again he dove, putting some distance between himself and the monster, springing back up to his feet while firing his final magazine. His last thirty bullets hit home but did nothing to slow The Evil down.

Do stood up and pulled out his last grenade. He backed up, calling for it to come to him, to finish him off. The Evil stood fully erect, its serpent tongue licking its lips. It smiled at him with its horrible human teeth and did something that sent a chill down his spine.

It spoke.

"No," it hissed with a grin that grew larger and ghastlier. Its attention turned to Nhat, who was struggling to run on the sand. "I want to reunite her with her family." It began stomping menacingly towards Nhat, who let out a piercing scream.

"NO!" Do shouted and pulled the pin from his grenade, running and launching it straight at The Evil's back. It hit and exploded, sending the creature tumbling forward, roaring in the predawn night. Do looked at his watch, *three minutes*. He looked to the east and saw the edges of the dark blue sky burning in purple. It was almost here, almost daylight. He drew his knife and charged at the beast. They were too close. *She* was too close. He and The Evil were going to die this morning.

A surge of energy overcame him as he sprinted full force at the gigantic beast, which was already back up and lumbering toward the girl with the pleasure of a sadistic madman. With his blade in hand, he lunged at its leg, grabbing onto the tree trunk-like appendage and drove the knife into it.

The Evil roared, looked down and swiped at Do. Do took the hit and tumbled into the sand. Savagery overtook him and he bolted up and attacked its leg again, slashing repeatedly and dodging as it swatted at him.

Leaping for the other leg, Do slammed into it with all his might and started slashing. Chunks of flesh flew away with each swing, forcing The Evil to turn around and swipe again. This time Do was ready, latching onto its arm as it flew past and began hacking away at it. Big hunks of its flesh fell to the sand, where they quickly burned away into nothing.

Do let go of the arm, falling to the ground in time to see the purple horizon turn orange. The sun was finally arriving; Do just had to keep fighting.

The Evil bent down to pick him up, but Do ran straight into the creature's claws and sliced at where its talons met its flesh. The monster recoiled and turned instead, slamming its tail straight into Do's body. He tumbled a few meters and landed on his back, sand in his face and eyes. He looked up to see The Evil heading straight towards Nhat, who nervously stood at the water's edge. Do screamed to her.

"GO! Swim!"

She looked to him and said something he couldn't hear.

"Swim! It's the only way out! There's no other way!"

The Evil lowered its body and began to chase after her on all of its legs. Seeing the beast come after her, Nhat turned to the water and began to wade into it. Her little legs raised over the waves as they landed, her face with horror at the unimaginable monster tearing after her. Sand flew into the air as if bombs were exploding underneath The Evil's feat. Do managed to get up and tear after it as well, sending plumes of sand up behind him. His boots heavy with sand, legs sore from a day and night of running, and his soul weary from it all.

As he sprinted, he saw Nhat make it to where the waves crashed and went under. He almost made a beeline for the water when he saw her come up and begin to swim. The light in the distance began to crest; he could see Naval vessels in the distance. It boiled down to seconds now, and he was going to use them all.

Too far from The Evil, he flipped his blade and grabbed the black metal. He stopped and aimed, throwing the knife with all his might at the beast who had imprisoned the souls of those he killed and those killed in the war that had cost him everything.

The knife pierced the nape of the beast's neck. It stopped and howled, clawing at the protruding blade.

Do ran at it, armed now with nothing but his bare hands as weapons. He tackled the closest leg with full force, managing to bring the beast down. Climbing on top of it, he began tearing away bits of its flesh, clawing like an animal at the monster that had hunted him. The Evil grabbed him, but Do bit into its claws, spitting out chunks of its matter and going back for more.

The creature tightened its grip further, and Do cried out in pain. Ignoring the agony, he continued to tear away flesh with his bare hands, releasing his rage against the horrible monster. The Evil tightened its grip further still and opened its gaping mouth, roaring at Do. Despite the ringing in his ears, he persisted, clawing at the creature's flesh until chunks of it hit the sand below, erupting into flames as he freed the trapped souls.

The Evil lifted him up and unhinged its jaws to swallow him again. Despite the imminent danger, Do continued to fight, his gaze shifting between Nhat, swimming far out in the water, and the breathtaking sunrise on the horizon.

Flames erupted around him as The Evil was engulfed, but it was hell bent on destroying the man who had cost it its wicked life. With a sense of peace washing over him, Do closed his eyes and surrendered to his fate, a smile gracing his lips as the creature brought him closer to its gaping mouth. He thought of Nhat and hoped that she would make it to her family in Paris, and quickly decided that yes, she would. Then, his mind turned to his own family, wondering if he would see his brother again and if they would be able to live the life that could have been.

Withstanding

Nhat had never been on a boat before, much less a battleship.

They found her floating in the South China Sea, holding onto her bag for dear life. She was twenty-four kilometers out to sea—a marvel for a grown man or woman, and an outright miracle for a child.

She didn't know who pulled her up or how long she had been unconscious. All she knew was that she was on an American ship and a lone Vietnamese lady had been taking care of her. To Nhat she looked very pretty but, like everyone else on the ship, very sad as well.

The woman took Nhat on walks around the ship when she recovered. They marveled at the strange new sights, and the woman told her that everything was going to be alright.

When Nhat first came to, she remembered her bag and the important things in it. The woman had saved everything for her and made sure it was all dry and intact.

She then remembered Do, and The Evil. She thought about telling the woman about it but decided against it, believing she would not understand. She looked around the ship during their walks for the man who helped her escape the terrible thing that had been hunting her, that had killed her family, but she never found him.

She would often go to the bow of the ship and look at the distant coastline, hoping that she would see him swimming out to meet them, or that when a boat made it to their ship she would see him among the soldiers who made it out when the communists took over.

Communists. That's what the woman told her the enemy was called. She had never heard her dad say anything about that in front of her. Then again, her dad always had his "grown up" talks locked in his office, or after she had gone to bed. She was sure she'd heard the word before, but until then, she was just a kid playing and doing kid things. She never had to learn grown up things until now.

186

Nhat was awfully quiet, drawing concern from the woman who was watching over her. Despite the woman's attempts to engage her in conversation, Nhat always responded with timid replies or subtle gestures.

It was dawn, and Nhat found herself once again at the ship's bow, looking for Do. The woman joined her, trying once again to learn more about this little girl who swam twenty-four kilometers out to sea.

"What are you looking at?" the pretty woman inquired, her fingers gently combing through Nhat's long black hair.

"The ocean." Nhat replied softly. She was practically swimming in an oversized US Navy t-shirt, finally looking again like a child and not a ragged wild thing fleeing a monster.

"Well, this isn't the ocean," the woman corrected gently, wrapping her arm around Nhat and drawing her closer. "It's the sea."

"The sea?" Nhat echoed.

"Mmm-hmm. It's a smaller part of the ocean," the woman explained, tossing her own long black hair back. "The ocean is gigantic, but this area is surrounded by islands, which are other countries, so it's considered a sea. Do you like the sea and ocean?" she prompted, happy that Nhat was opening up a bit.

Nhat nodded. "I do."

"What do you like about it?"

"The water," Nhat replied simply.

"What about the water do you like?" the woman pressed gently, stroking Nhat's hair.

"The color, and how it looks," Nhat elaborated.

"And what specifically about this water do you like?" the woman persisted, careful not to overwhelm Nhat with too many questions.

Nhat fell silent. She didn't know how to articulate her feelings, so she shrugged.

Respecting Nhat's silence, the woman waited patiently for her to answer the question. When it was clear that she wasn't going to, the woman asked her another, giving Nhat another opportunity to express herself.

"Well, if you could use just one word to describe this sea, what would it be?" she asked gently.

Nhat looked up at her and then out to the sea. She thought about the way the water looked, the clarity of the sea and how she could see fish swimming at the beach when she went with her family. How pretty it

187

looked right now, and that even though it was dark blue in the early light, she could still see how clear it was and how deep it went.

Nhat made a noise to let the woman know that she was thinking, like she would at school when her teacher asked her a question. She looked out again. If Do were to swim up to the ship she would see him. She thought about all the books she read with her dad. All the games she played with her mom. All the big words her brother used because he was so smart.

Nhat looked up at the woman with quiet determination. "I think I have one," she said tentatively.

"Go ahead, then," the woman encouraged, smiling warmly at Nhat. "What's the one word you would use to describe something so beautiful?"

"Crystal."